MW01098993

C. S. Peter

Broken Compass

September 2018

Broken Compass

C. S. Petersen

Petersen Publishing

Broken Compass

This is a work of fiction. All names, characters, locales, and incidents are products of the author's imagination and any resemblance to actual people, places, or events is coincidental or fictionalized.

Published in Canada 2018 by Petersen Publishing

Second Edition

ISBN-13: 9780995863927
ISBN-10: 099586392X

For my friends and family, who always encouraged me to keep writing. May there always be a story out there to be heard.

Acknowledgements

I have a lot of people to thank for the existence of this book. Truthfully, this book was written as a project for Creative Writing class in school, but because my teacher for this class is so amazing, I decided to take it a step further and publish the book so that the final product is memorable for her. I hope that everyone has someone in their life who can be a mentor in the way that this teacher has been to me.

It's also due to all my friends and family who stood by me throughout this entire project, helping me along the way by being Beta Readers, Editors, Designers, and just all-around givers of feedback on all my ideas. It helped to shape this piece of work into what it is and whenever I look back on it, I'll always remember the effort we put into it together.

CHAPTER I

On any typical day, the sun would fall over a land from the moment it rose to the moment it fell, spreading its warmth and light over all on the earth below. However, the city of Arbane – the very heart of the kingdom of Ghanara – was surrounded by high walls, so many of the buildings were shrouded in shadow for the better part of each day. The marketplace, a bustling stretch of street vendors' stands and storefronts down the main stretch of road, was always bright, for the long shadows of the barrier walls did not reach it, no matter the height of the sun in the sky. This was both a relief and a discomfort, for the light provided the busy shoppers with sight, but it also brought intense heat, which poured down upon them, especially in the summer months.

In the height of the hottest season, every shopper was glistening with sweat, their shirts clinging to their bodies. They swarmed the wide street which was too narrow to hold them, and they spilled into side streets as well. For many of them, their aim was to buy the fanciest headwrap to wear, the freshest fruit to eat, or to try the newest perfume to parade around with. The entire street left people entrapped in a cloud of exotic spices and the scent of fresh flowers and bread. The heavy atmosphere only helped them to ignore the sun's rays beating down upon their heads – the same sun that left their skin dark and their hair bleached for the better part of the year.

Unlike them, though, there were others in the crowd – ones who weren't just there to buy.

One such individual, a lanky sixteen-year-old lad by the name of Axel, snuck quickly through the crowd, his footsteps light on the packed dirt. Around him, city folk were pushing and shoving, as they were every day, to be the first to view the merchandise in the street vendors' stands. They didn't notice him as his hands wandered among their possessions, too focused on the wares in front of them to look back.

Ducking into a side street, Axel opened his hands in the shadow to examine his prizes. Only a few items stood out against the usual junk – a few copper coins, a cheap pocket watch from the scammer on the corner, the pit of a goldfruit tree. He sighed, closing his shimmering emerald eyes and leaning his head back against the brick and mortar wall of the cracked clay

CHAPTER I

hut behind him. Stuffing the items back in one of the many pockets littering his tunic, he leaned out to look into the crowd, his eyes searching for anything valuable to loot.

Then, a pair of guards marched past, causing Axel to duck his head back in behind the corner of the building, turtling his neck to stay out of sight. For boys like him, the guards meant bad news. They were always patrolling, ever-controlling from the orders of the emperor who ruled over the land. He was the one who had conquered the land from his predecessor and changed everything.

The tall, towering spires were built to surround the city in his name, for their "protection", he claimed. Axel called it a lie. He saw the truth. It was to keep them in line. The walls allowed for the guards' easy watch over them, long walkways all around the city for prying eyes to peer down at the city folk going about their business, not even feeling the eyes burning into their backs. Axel felt them. He felt them like insects crawling over his skin, like rats in his trousers, nipping and biting at his flesh in the most unpleasant ways.

He slipped back into the flow of the shoppers, this time keeping his hands to himself. Instead, Axel let his eyes wander continuously, from one end of the street, where the main gate stood as the only entrance and exit of the city, to the other, where the public fountain stood, wide and open for anyone to use.

This fountain, built around the narrow canal that ran through the city, was the freshest water that Axel had ever tasted, though, his opinion was biased, as it was the only water he had ever tasted. It ran from one end of the city to the other, splitting it in half and only curving to encircle the central palace. Because of this, there were multiple small bridges running over the water throughout the city, and usually, people swarmed around the edges of them. The traffic around these bridges was so dense that nearly every hour, at least one person would fall, resulting in a sudden splash. They, of course, would not receive help from the passers-by and would have to just move on, soaked.

As he passed a booth selling elegant silk scarves of various colours, Axel heard a shrill voice and turning, saw a rather large woman as she shuffled around, fussing over which scarf she wished to buy. She held three different pieces of silk in her hands, all the same shade of blue, but she was bumbling over her words, her cheeks puffed out as she asked continuous questions to the merchant, who just stared at her rather flustered.

Axel raised an eyebrow as the woman held up the darkest coloured scarf. "Do you know if this is mulberry silk or charmeuse silk? This is very important because I cannot stand charmeuse against my skin."

The merchant stuttered, "Miss, all our silks are mulberry, and are also charmeuse. I-it's the weave,

4

miss. Mulberry is the type of silk spun, but charmeuse is the weave we use."

Smiling at the woman's balked expression, Axel walked closer, bumping into her. Due to her obvious advantage in size, he was the one knocked back in the dirt. Scrambling to his feet to avoid being trampled, he quickly said, "'M sorry, miss, didn't see ya there."

She whirled around, the three scarves over her arm swishing gently from the momentum. "Get out of here, boy! It's not like you could afford any of these items, anyway!" she sneered at him, her tone lashing like poison off her tongue.

Axel bowed his head and retreated, but as he turned away, he grinned secretly, for in his hand was a rather large polished golden ring that he'd slipped from around her swollen finger. He dashed away, lost in the crowd once again before she would notice her missing possession. Slipping into a back alley, Axel maneuvered through the back roads, over the crates and barrels that had been discarded once they had outlived their usefulness. In a way, Axel could relate to the various items he found on these roads, cast away pieces of trash, unwanted by society – just like himself. He took a special route, one that only he and his friends knew through the abandoned, darkened alleys of Arbane.

After one final corner, he reached an old warehouse on the east edge of town. This building had been abandoned due to instabilities in the surrounding lands, so until the sinkholes were filled, all construction attempts were put on hold. It seemed indefinite as the emperor wouldn't spare a single copper piece for such a project.

Across the large metal double-doors of the warehouse were long, scuffed boards in an X formation; the windows were covered in a similar fashion. Axel quickly ran along the side of the warehouse, dodging half-hung linens and stacks of wooden beams. As natural as breathing, Axel weaved through the obstacles and entered the building through an entrance on the side. It wasn't really an entrance, just a section of the building where the wall had been chipped open to provide access to the interior.

He ducked inside, walking through the darkened hallways. He passed lean-tos of boards; the smell of old mortar filled his nose as he darted around open barrels. He kept moving until he reached an open section of the warehouse, directly in the centre. It was filled with people, about thirty or so, all dressed similarly to Axel, with old patched tunics, ruffled trousers and bare feet that were stained with the speckled red mud of Arbane.

Just as he arrived, he saw Joshua, the leader of their family, standing on a podium at the front of the room, about to begin a meeting. He was a lanky man, just like Axel, and he had a dirty face, but most of the time he wore a wide grin and his crisp blue eyes were constantly sparkling. On his chin, his grizzly beard wobbled as he spoke.

"My friends, welcome! All of you are here as our friends, but most importantly, you are family. We took you in when you had nowhere else to go. We provide for each other, which leads me to the reason for this meeting. Our next big steal will be on the emperor himself! He's been sitting on his throne as a lazy loiter-sack for too long! He thinks that just because he has a little necklace 'round his scrag that he can control us, but I say: Nay! We'll show him we're not his sheep!"

As Joshua shouted his words of inspiration, a roar of agreement erupted from the assembled people. Axel pushed his way to the front to get a better view.

"Now get in line, ya scoundrels! I'll be assigning jobs for ya! Ev'ryone gets a job, an' if ev'ryone plays their part, we'll be in and out in a jiffy!"

Movement commenced as the others surged forward, eager to receive their role. Unable to resist the flow, Axel was washed along with the mass of bodies. Finally, it stopped, and he regained his balance. Near him were three of his friends.

"Hey Angie, hey Jackie," he greeted the twins. Angie was the nicest girl his age that he'd ever met, and Axel would be lying if he said he didn't have a crush on her when he was younger. Her brother, Jackie, was the older of the two, but he didn't show it, usually being protected by Angie whenever a fight broke out. The third person was Marco, who was a little older than the three of them, around twenty-five, but he never knew his parents, so he couldn't recount his age precisely.

As they were waiting in line, Angie said, "So, how about the palace, huh? I've never been there, myself, but I've heard that it's bigger on the inside than the outside and it's so hard to navigate. Can't wait to see it."

Axel scowled. The expression was one he hated, for it wrinkled his eyes together and his forehead was a maze of edges, but it was the only expression he could convey at the mention of the palace. "I 'ate that place! Anythin' ta do with the emperor stinks! If I had a choice, I'd burn it all down!"

"Which is why we're robbin' 'im. Obviously, he spends way too much of our money on his own life's joy," Jackie grumbled, worrying his lip as it came closer and closer to his turn for a role.

"I know he killed your parents, but it's not all bad. They loved you very much and now you got us, so...you turned out alright!" Angie said, her tone chipper. The smile she cast his way was brilliant. It seemed that the sun had snuck inside to grace them with its presence.

Unfortunately, he did know better. They were, as always, in the dark, their lives and their houses only lit by dim lamps strewn around, always running out of the meagre oil they were able to scrounge or steal whenever the opportunity was there.

Axel frowned, the corners of his mouth sinking nearly to his chin, but once Angie wrapped her arms around him in a tight hug, he smiled, melting into her embrace. Pulling away only seconds later, he reached into the pocket of his frayed trousers to retrieve his most prized possession – a compass, once silver, was rusted and dirty after years of use, but still perfect in his eyes. Flipping it open, he smiled at the thin needle as it wobbled midway between north and west. The compass was usually off by a few degrees, but it didn't matter.

Then, he turned his eyes to the other side, and his smile grew as he saw the tiny picture that had been stuffed into the small indent in the case. It was a sketch that an artist had done for him and his family when he was very small – when his parents were still alive. He couldn't remember much of them, but he remembered being so fussy when the artist had positioned him just so, trying to get the perfect angle for such a tiny piece of art.

The three of them sat, smiling at the artist in the sketch, but every time Axel looked at the picture, he focused on his parents' smiles, picturing that they knew he was looking at the image and were smiling for him and him alone. He always remembered that day with a bittersweet smile because he'd never been able to sit still, and he'd hated the entire experience, claiming loudly that he'd never get another picture done.

Now, he wanted nothing more than to go back, even to that place, if only to be with his parents again. Overall, he was glad that he'd struggled through the sitting because at least he had something to remember his mother and father by.

Snapping the compass closed with a sudden click, he looked up with determination as Joshua beckoned him forward. Jaw set, and eyes held firm, Axel stepped forward, prepared to receive his job. With a nod, he said, "I'm ready."

CHAPTER II

Shortly after receiving his assignment, Axel moved into position.

He was to be a lookout, which gave a plain view of everyone as they also got into their places. In the back of his mind, a whisper of thought told him how similar their heist was to the plays that used to go on at the grand theatre in the north quarter of the city.

Once the stage was set, the performance would begin, and anything could happen. At least, before the emperor had closed the place down, claiming that it "spread nothing but lies". That had been done six years ago.

Axel squatted near the raised barrier on the roof of one of the higher buildings near the palace, staying low enough to not raise attention, and just in the shadows of the even higher wall that bordered the courtyard. From this height, he could just smell the wafting snips of aroma from the marketplace in sparse drifts of wind, and as many other places in the city, it was pleasantly dark where he sat.

He could see a few of his friends – Marco, Jackie, and Angie included – and used the small piece of a broken mirror to signal to them in Morse code. "C.O.A.S.T.I.S.C.L.E.A.R," he signalled. After two more repetitions, he stopped, putting the mirror upside down next to him. Then, he ducked behind a few burlap sacks and poorly built wooden crates that were stored there, keeping an eye out from the small space between two of the large crates. Being as small as he was, he could squeeze right in between the packs and the cases, camouflaged in the dull mess with his muted clothes and dirt-filled hair.

His friends – as was their assignment - received his message, and in turn, they sent it to the gang members who were physically going in to rob the palace. Three groups of three were dispatched, Joshua leading one, Marco leading the second, and another older member named Arabella leading the third. They entered, knocking out the guards quickly and quietly without raising any alarms.

For a while, the heist was going along smoothly, but there was always something that would go obscenely wrong. Somewhere, somehow, the guards had been alerted. Maybe an alarm was raised, maybe they were seen – it mattered not because right at that moment,

CHAPTER II

Axel heard the shouting start. Everything was suddenly in motion as the gang members scrambled from their positions, trying desperately to get away when the guards pulled back their covers and grabbed them by the collars, hustling them along toward the palace.

In the courtyard, more guards flooded through the doors, dressed head to toe in finely polished chainmail and armed with swords or spears. They wielded their weapons dangerously, warding off the city folk as they hunted their prey. Axel wanted to help – really, he did, but every instinct within him told him to hide, to blend in, so that was what he did. Even as his friends – his family – were being dragged off to the dungeons, he crouched low and stayed where he was, his greyish-brown street clothes helping him more than ever to camouflage against the burlap sacks of grain that remained huddled around him.

Footsteps thundered toward him. He could hear them on the stairs. Each step sent a jolt through his chest, his heart fluttering within his ribcage like a trapped bird, and all he could do was hope that they didn't catch him because of it. When the guards reached the roof, they passed him without even noticing.

"It's all clear!" one yelled, "Let's keep moving!"

And then they were gone.

Down below, Axel heard a shout of "Over here!" and couldn't help but peek over the ledge. To his horror, Angie and Jackie were dragged from their hiding places and thrown to the dirt. They were inspected, and then, with a single nod, they were taken away to the dungeons along with everyone else.

Soon, the moment of chaos was over, and Axel was left alone in the calm and the quiet. Within him, though, it was neither of those things. His heart was still racing, and there was a throbbing in his skull, but he could not stop it no matter how hard he tried to focus on calming thoughts. He knew just by looking at the guards dragging away his friends that some had escaped, but they most likely fled the city, never to return, or would be caught at a later date. He knew that he'd have to move eventually, but even though he was ninety percent sure it was safe, Axel remained where he was, huddled with his arms around his legs and his face buried in his knees. Everyone he knew was gone.

*

Finally, after what felt like hours, Axel moved. Struggling to stand with his sore muscles and stiff limbs, he looked over the edge of the building cautiously. His heart sank. In the courtyard – or at least, what little he could see of it – was everyone he ever knew, standing, lined up like targets. They were all in chains, ankles, and wrists bound as they shuffled in their places. They were awaiting their fate to be decided, but Axel and everyone else knew what it would be. There was no surprise. Only suspense before the words were actually said.

On the balcony above was the emperor, sneering down at them. His dark hair shone in the direct sunlight, while his clean-shaven chin gleamed. Around his neck, amidst the rich purple fabric of his robes and shiny golden jewelry, a single accessory stood out: an old-looking medallion, which glowed with a mysterious black light, as if it held shadows within.

He was quiet for a while as if considering the people before him carefully, though Axel was certain that there were no thoughts other than malice running through his head at all. Then, he spoke the words that Axel was dreading to hear more than any other.

"For committing treason against the crown, I am left with no choice but to sentence you all to death!" he announced. "At dawn tomorrow, your leader shall be beheaded in the courtyard. May his fate be an example to all who come after!" He studied Joshua for a moment, who stood at the front of the crowd, his posture perfectly straight and stiff despite the heavy chains binding him in place.

"I beg to differ!" Joshua cried out in defiance, his voice strong. "Let me be a martyr to ev'ryone else! I will not die in vain, 'cause now, if they don't already, the people will see you as you truly are: a maniacal tyrant! Yer the sickness of this land, and if we're gonna get better, we need ta get rid of ya! Down with the emperor!"

The gang members began chanting, "Down with the emperor! Down with the emperor! Down with the emperor!" but they were immediately silenced by the guards, who sent most of them to the brick-laden ground with firm punches and quick shoves.

Glancing back at the emperor, Axel felt the dread in his heart grow stronger as he saw how much the man's expression darkened in the wake of Joshua's speech. His cruel, beady eyes glinted with malevolence. "We will not wait until tomorrow! Chop off his head, now!" The command was firm, with no room for discussion, and just the tone sent shivers up and down Axel's spine. He couldn't possibly imagine how it was to be in the courtyard.

The guards forced Joshua to his knees, their leather gloved hands giving them a fair grip on his bare arms. They held him in place as a third guard drew his sword and unceremoniously lobbed Joshua's head clean off his shoulders. It hit the ground with a dull thunk and rolled, causing many to grimace. Joshua's body fell limp, the top half already becoming soaked in his blood.

"Take them away," the emperor said nonchalantly, waving his hand towards the rest of the prisoners. "They shall die later tonight."

CHAPTER II

In a single file line, each member of the gang that Axel had grown up with was led away to their deaths. They were brought down to the dungeons to live their final moments in a dank, dirty cell and then killed in the harshest of ways, forced to watch their friends before them, and carrying the heavy knowledge that their friends would have to watch them die as well.

Throughout the night, their screams were heard throughout the city, only dulled by the thick layers of brick and dirt that separated the dungeons from the fresh air. By morning, there was nothing but silence, and Axel felt a seed of guilt settle deep within his chest. He had survived while the others had not.

It was well after dark on the second night when he finally moved from where he had tucked himself away. He'd had time to think, and now, he only knew one thing: he had to get revenge for his family and friends. It was as if he could still hear their screams in his head, begging for their deaths to not go in vain.

Now, Axel didn't know what he could do, but all he wanted to do was make the emperor's life as hard as possible, which he knew would be a lot of work. The first thing to do, at least in Axel's mind, was to disrupt the guards' work. If he took down the emperor's main enforcers, then maybe life would be easier for him and everyone else in the city.

And thus, his pranks began.

Using his small frame and lanky body to sneak around easily, he started leaving "gifts" for the guards to find. He left many buckets of water to fall on them as they opened doors. He greased up the stones on the paths, causing them to slip. One guard even ended up falling into the half-moat around the castle, and for the whole day, was struggling to climb out. That one left Axel in stitches. Unfortunately, a guard must've heard him, because he turned to look, and saw Axel tucked in the alley between two huts a little down the road.

"You! Boy! Stop laughing!" he commanded, waving a leather-enwrapped hand jerkily to enforce his words.

Axel did not. In hindsight, he should have and just continued with his day, but it was just too funny.

"That's it! Get him!" the guard yelled, and seconds later, Axel found himself running for his life, tailed by three, large, armour-donned men. He easily took the lead, being small and fast and generally aerodynamic, while the guards were weighed down by their muscle, their chainmail, and their weapons, but they were slowly gaining on him.

Underneath him, his feet hit the packed dirt, each step a split second of contact before he was back in the air, almost flying down the streets. He turned left and found himself in the marketplace again. Pausing for only a moment, Axel darted between two people as the whole crowd rolled like a wave on the coast. Just before he got lost in this wave, though, he felt a sudden burn in his thigh. His whole muscle strained, feeling hot and cold at the same time and when Axel looked down, he paled as he saw a small knife hilt hanging, suspended from the back of his leg.

He stumbled, the pain coming seconds later in a tremendous sweep. Instead of going straight as he'd originally planned, he hobbled forward, angling to a side street as his method of escape. He slipped in without anyone noticing and slid behind a large stack of rugs that one vendor kept out of sight until he would set up again with new merchandise. Sliding down the wall, Axel looked at his leg. The knife's blade was completely buried within his flesh, luckily, so that there was no blood trail leading the guards directly to him, but it still hurt like hell.

The hilt mocked him as he stared at it, debating whether to take it out or just leave it in. He'd have to do so eventually, but if he did, he'd most likely just bleed out in this alley. His mind made itself up, suddenly telling him to grab the hilt and pull, wiggling it back and forth to try and pry it out. A hiss escaped his lips as he clenched his teeth, nearly biting through the surface skin of his tongue to keep himself from screaming, because the blade had struck bone and he was trying to wrench iron from its new home in his tibia.

Once he managed to pry it loose, his hand wrapped around the bloody injury almost immediately, keeping some pressure on the wound. With on hand, he grabbed a strip of fabric that he'd torn off the bottom edge of his tunic and wrapped it tightly, binding the flesh together. Using the wall to stand, he hobbled down the side street, about to turn the next bend when a voice cried out, "There he is!"

The guards had found him.

"After him!" another yelled, and more footsteps thundered behind him.

With a rush of adrenaline, Axel pushed forward, speeding up into a jog, though his limp was still present. He darted down the street, his pace slowing with every step, and he wasn't sure if he'd ever make it out alive.

CHAPTER III

The morning after the executions, an architect and his daughter grew more and more worried for their safety. As the ex-royal architect, the man – Tobias – was on the list of people the guards found suspicious. When he'd left, he hadn't even given the emperor warning. No letter of notice had been sent, nor was a replacement found. It had been almost fifteen years and yet, the position remained empty, so the emperor allowed the city to fall slowly to ruins with no one to rebuild it.

Not only were the rougher parts of town only getting rougher over the years, even the nicer streets – especially the ones closest to the palace – were becoming worn. Only the rich and important could afford a personal architect and builders to design and renovate their homes.

Since he quit, Tobias and his wife, Maria, left their grand apartment in the light of the courtyard to live in a small hut a few streets down from the marketplace, out of the limelight – and most importantly, out of the way of the guard's regular patrol routes. Soon after, their daughter was born, but despite the efforts of their midwife, Maria's life was forfeit for the life of young Meredith, as named by Maria's final breath.

She was born early, and barely survived herself, but Tobias was determined. His wife had died to give his little angel the chance to live, so he'd do anything and everything in his power to make sure she took advantage of that chance, and had the best, most luxurious life he could provide. Her education would be held in high regard in their household, with her lessons beginning as soon as she was old enough to sit up on her own and private tutors arriving at their house as long as he could afford them.

And, although faced with the hardships of raising his child alone, Tobias managed with the care and kindness of his friends, though they too, left him over the years. Ten years after his wife's death, he and his daughter were alone, with only each other to battle the loneliness.

*

Tobias entered the marketplace, his calloused hand holding tight to his daughter's smaller, smoother one as they wandered, keeping their eyes out for the stand that sold ink. He was running low and knew that as someone in his position, it would be disastrous to run out of ink even for a day.

Though his daughter hid her face in her hair when they walked, Tobias was delighted that he'd brought her along. She rarely got out of the house, preferring to bury herself in the dark shelter of their hut with her nose in one of the many books that littered their living quarters. He often joked that she was a hermit without her cave and she'd laughed right along, but as soon as she was outside the safety of their home, she closed off from the world, frightened like a clam from one of the coastal market stands.

Sometimes, she would only leave the house when he forced her to accompany him on his errands, because the gods above knew that she only ever left their house on her own to look at the stars from the roof. Never had she willingly gone out on her own when the sun was high in the sky.

"Come on, Meredith; let's pass by these people. Politely now," Tobias told his daughter, and the two of them passed a large group of women who were standing around the stand of fresh exotic fruit from the eastern coastal market.

"'Scuse us," Meredith said in a small voice as they passed. She looked up, squinting at the sky and then ducked her head as she saw the sun peaking over the east wall. Letting her hair fall in front of her face, she kept her face tilted to the ground, hiding it in from the bright glow of the morning sun. As if to spite her, the sun kissed her pale cheeks, making them gleam in an almost heavenly hue.

They passed the stand for scarves, the stand for southern spices, and the stand for fresh, top quality parchment – which was also extremely expensive, Tobias thought – and finally came to the stand with pots of ink, a variety of quills, and small bags of sand straight from the Uvian desert.

"What can I get'cha?" the vendor asked, leaning over the back of his stand and grinning at the two of them. He was a young man, possibly in his early twenties, and had a messy mop of hair on his head under a floppy hat. As he breathed, there was a slight whistle where air escaped between the gaps in his chipped front teeth.

"Just two pots of ink, please," the architect replied, passing over two silver coins and eight copper ones. Both were stamped flat with images on both sides, though were uneven in their edges. Some were often larger than others, and the stamps weren't always centered.

"Seems like you've done this before," the vendor joked as he took the coins. "Bet'cha saw my father a lot."

"Yes," Tobias replied politely, "How is he?"

CHAPTER III

Meredith shuffled a little behind him, hiding her face a little more. She didn't like it when her father made conversation. She preferred that he just go about his business and let them go back home. Scowling at the hard-packed ground, she thought of all the other, worthwhile things she could be doing. Like reading; the thought crossed her mind swiftly, though lingered long enough to elicit a soft grumble from the girl.

The vendor shrugged. "He's not bad. A little sick right now, but he'll live. We've got him the right medicine from Brenda down there," the boy pointed down the street. With his ink-splattered fingers, he went to hand over two bottles of ink, but paused, "No, wait," he muttered, putting down one of the pots. "That's for display: empty. Here," he handed Tobias a different pot. "Sorry, I haven't done this in a while. Got my own thing goin' fer now. Pottery: my passion. Some things just click, ya know?"

"Yes, I hear you." Tobias gave a chuckle. "Thank you; take care of your father now, okay?" he said, glancing down at the merchandise and smiling up at the vendor, who smiled back, once again showing off his uneven, chipped teeth.

"My pleasure, and I will. You come back now, right? We got the best ink in town!"

After being satisfied with his product, Tobias took his daughter's hand once more and the two of them headed over to another stand – one which was laden with hats. "Would you like one, darling?" Tobias asked, looking down at her. Crinkles formed around his eyes, though his smile held nothing but dear affection for his beautiful girl.

"No thank you, dad," she replied softly.

"Alright. Then let's go home," he replied, and together, the two of them walked home, unaware of the desperate boy who had just entered the marketplace, followed closely by the guards.

CHAPTER IV

Axel felt fingertips on the back of his tunic as he turned another corner.The fear of being caught caused him to spring forward a couple more steps. Up ahead, he saw a fence, and he vaulted up onto a stack of crates, which wobble under his feet. With another desperate leap, he was over the fence. A jolt was sent up his legs as soon as he landed, and though he made sure to only make contact with his good leg, the pain that rushed through him caused his vision to blacken and his body to fall. On the other side, the stack of crates collapsed as well, arousing a cloud of dust, blocking the guards from following him.

Knowing the city, Axel suspected that the guards would find another way to get him; they seemed determined. He turned another corner, and, in his haste, forgot that it led to a dead end. His feet stuttered to a stop, skidding slightly in the dirt. Head swishing from left to right, he searched desperately for another exit, for he knew that if he went back the same way, he'd surely meet the guards.

Then, to his left, like his prayers had been answered, a door opened, and a hand extended, beckoning him inside. "Come on! This way!" a quiet, female voice hissed.

Axel sighed in relief as he darted towards the door. He hadn't even seen it, hidden behind crates filled with rain-soaked scrolls. They were old and wet and kind of gross-looking. As soon as Axel was inside, a large hand grabbed his shoulder and yanked him further inside so that the door could be closed behind him. He was led into a living room, though it wasn't much for "living". There was a single chair and a single, low table, and the floor was lined with stacks of books, some old and dusty while others were well-used and dust-free; they obviously had been thumbed through often. The table also held books, but also parchment, quills, an ink pot, and a lit oil lamp.

"Dad, I'll stay with him while you go get some first aid supplies," said a girl that seemed to be only slightly younger than Axel. She had a young, babyish face with an innocent, aloof smile and her pale skin glowed almost angelically in the light of the yellow flames.

The man nodded, leaving the room without a word.

CHAPTER IV

"Here, sit down," the girl said, motioning to the chair for Axel to rest in. He gladly took advantage of the offer, falling back into the soft material and stretching his legs out, one longer than the other. Wincing slightly, he relaxed his left foot, stretching out his toes. They were blackened from many years of him running around without any shoes to cover them. The bottoms were calloused and at least three shades darker than the rest of his body.

The girl smiled as he sat and then plopped down on the floor herself, lying on her stomach as she pulled a book closer to her and flipped it open to a page somewhere in the middle. Peeking at it, Axel saw a few star maps and a mess of written scribbles that he assumed were words, but then again, he had never learned to read. And even though she seemed to be focusing on the words, Axel saw that her eyes were still on him, watching carefully.

"Who are ya?" he asked after a moment of listening to the girl hum a tune to herself as she read.

"I'm Meredith," she told him, looking up only to meet his eyes for a moment before returning her gaze to her book.

"Why'd ya help me?" he asked. His tone was harsh and accusing, eyes narrowed as he glared at the suspicious man and strange girl that had taken him into their house.

"We just saved your life," another voice came from the hall. It was the man. "You ought to be more grateful. Unless you wanted to be caught by those guards." The man walked in and knelt next to the chair where Axel sat, opening a white case. Inside were bandages and a long, thin bottle of alcohol.

After setting the supplies down, the man began to unwrap the fabric from around Axel's lower leg, which was sticky and crusty from the blood.

"My name is Tobias, and I see you've already met my daughter," the man introduced himself as he set the bloody strip aside. He then opened the bottle of alcohol and soaked a strip of fresh gauze in it. "This may sting a little," he warned.

Axel nodded, so Tobias poured the alcohol over the wound, then quickly pressed the gauze to his leg and began rubbing gently to clean the wound.

Before Axel had the chance to scream, Meredith jumped up and grabbed another wad of gauze, stuffing it into his mouth. "Shh!" she hissed, "You don't want to alert the guards!"

Axel nodded, biting down on the gauze and clenching his eyes shut, tears forming in the corners. Shivers ran throughout his whole body as Tobias continued to clean the wound, dabbing it with more and more gauze until finally, he deemed it sanitized enough to rewrap, which he did, almost perfectly. After he was done, he packed up his materials and stood to put them away and dispose of the bloody gauze, once again leaving Axel and Meredith alone in the living room.

Axel spit the makeshift gag out of his mouth. "What was tha' abou'?" he demanded. "That burned like mad!"

"We had to sterilize the wound," Meredith explained, shrugging.

"Can't let you get an infection now, can we?" Tobias asked as he re-entered the room.

Meredith scooted forward on the floor. "What were they chasing you for?" she asked, intrigued.

Axel's face split into a grin. "I got 'em soaked! Sen' one guard tumbling into the moat and 'e spen' all day tryin' ta get out but couldn't! Ha! Best prank ever!"

Tobias' eyebrow arched questioningly. "And what were you doing playing pranks on the guards?" he asked in the most apparent dad-voice that Axel had ever heard.

The boy shrugged. "I wan' their lives as bad as mine has been. Might as well have 'em shiverin' while they mess up other people's days," he explained, "Their damned master has 'emheelin' at 'is feet, an' after what 'e did, I can't forgive 'im."

Tobias sighed. "They can't help it. The emperor is using a magical amulet to hypnotize them. As the palace guards, he has more contact with them than any other person in town, so his influence over them is stronger, even at great distances. They're just his puppets at this point," he said, his tone melancholy. In his eyes, there was a faraway look, and he seemed lost in his memories as he spoke. Memories of what, Axel didn't know.

"I think I seen it b'fore. Back when 'e was up there sentencin' ma friend ta death. What'd ya know about it?" Axel asked, eyeing him suspiciously.

"I used to work at the palace as the royal architect," Tobias explained, gesturing to the many scrolls around the room, which Axel realized at that moment were old blueprints. "When Absinthe first took over as emperor from his predecessor, it was a little strange, but that was to be expected. Then, after a few weeks, I noticed some of my friends – the guards, I mean – were acting differently. Looking into it, I found out the truth and quit without a second thought. I moved into this house and shortly after, Meredith was born. We've lived here ever since."

Axel nodded.

"I think the only way to save them is to destroy the amulet. If it's gone, the emperor won't have anything to control them with anymore. Then I'm sure the people will rebel because his control over them will be broken. He's a terrible ruler anyway."

CHAPTER IV

"I want 'im off that throne of 'is, so how do we destroy the amulet?"

"Why do you hate him so much?" Meredith asked suddenly.

"Meredith!" Tobias scolded. "You don't ask questions like that!"

Meredith winced. "Sorry, dad."

"S'alright," Axel replied, "First, 'e killed ma parents. They didn't do nothin' and 'e offed 'em. Then, when I had nobody, Joshua took me in, and just yesterday they offed 'im, too!" He sniffled a little, a few tears welling in his eyes as he thought of the gang he'd grown up with. There was a hollowness in his chest where their warmth had once been. "I 'ad a home; now I 'ave nothin'."

"Well, if you want, you can stay with us for the time being. We'll figure something out, but you can't stay here long because if the guards find you, we're all dead," Tobias offered.

"Thanks." Axel smiled up at him.

Later, Axel was laying in the spare bed, just staring at the ceiling. He laid like that for most of the night, and he was sure that he'd memorized the texture of their ceiling by the time morning light began to shine through the drawn curtains over the small, misshapen window. Throughout the night, he couldn't sleep, for every time he closed his eyes, he saw his friends being dragged away. He heard their screams in his ears constantly, heard the sharp swing of the sword on Joshua's neck, slicing through his flesh.

His leg was propped up, but there was still a subtle throb, and he knew that he'd have to take it easy for the next few weeks – maybe a month –if it was going to heal at least decently.

It was only due to complete and utter exhaustion that he fell into a light slumber, only to be woken by the crowing of a cockerel outside his window. Sitting up in bed, he swung his legs over the edge, wincing once again as a twinge raced up his injured leg and directly into his spine. He sighed.

Axel reached into his pocket, ready to look at the picture of his parents – as he did every morning – only to find that his compass wasn't there. His heart rate spiked. "Where is it?" he mumbled quietly to himself, jumping out of bed and getting on the floor to look for it.

He searched the entire room, throwing things around until it was a complete mess, but he still couldn't find it.

"Whoa! What happened in here? Did you let loose some mad dogs?" Tobias cried as he opened the door, balancing a tray of food in one hand.

"I can't find it!" Axel cried, on his knees again as he checked under the bed for the seventh time.

CHAPTER IV

"Can't find what?" Tobias asked, setting the tray on the rumpled covers.

"Ma compass! I need ma compass! It's gotta be 'ere somewhere! I know I 'ad it!"

"Well, you did a lot of running around yesterday; maybe it fell out of your pocket then?" Tobias suggested.

Axel jumped to his feet, completely ignoring the sharp stinging sensation in his lower leg. "Yer a genius, mister! I've gotta go find it! Thanks for brekkie!" He grabbed a slice of bread and jam from the tray and darted out of the room before Tobias could get another word in.

Retracing his steps from the previous day, Axel found his compass in the alley with the rugs, just outside the market. It was still early, so there weren't as many people as the previous day, but there were still quite a bit considering the time. The compass caught his eye only because it was still shiny enough to catch the light, and he snatched it up without a second thought, running back to Tobias' hut. His limp was extremely noticeable, so his run was more of a hop-skip-hobble of movement in the dark.

His fingers rubbed over the surface of the compass almost instinctively as he tried to get rid of the dirt on his way back. He was just about to turn the corner again when he heard a loud shout coming from the front gate of the palace courtyard. Interest piqued and self-preservation skills suddenly absent, Axel decided to investigate.

There, at the front gate, the two guards were having the life beaten out of them by a mysterious figure dressed all in black. The stranger moved with inhuman grace, dodging and landing hits with the speed of a cheetah and the grace of a gazelle as it pranced through the plains. Axel always loved watching the gazelles as they ran; he watched them from the castle walls whenever he managed to sneak to the top of them without being spotted. However, this stranger was something else entirely.

With a sudden jerk of his hand, a guard ripped off the figure's hood, revealing her face. Yes, her. It was a woman, fighting the guards and winning. Directly after they unmasked her, she knocked them out, but it was too late. As she was occupied, a third guard snuck up on her and used her preoccupation with his two co-workers to his advantage, knocking her around the head with the butt of his sword.

She fell to the ground, unconscious, and he dragged her inside, most likely to the dungeons to await the emperor deciding her fate. It would be another execution, for sure.

"I gotta 'elp 'er," Axel whispered to himself. "Anyone who messes with them guards is okay in ma books."

CHAPTER IV

Sneaking forward, he pulled the unconscious guards into the alley and stole their uniforms, then dumped them into the back of a cart of flour sacks as it left the city for trading in the eastern market on the coast.

He laughed quietly to himself as he thought about them waking up, confused and in nothing but their braies in the back of a cart.

Surely, it would be many miles before they woke, and they'd have to travel all the way back to the city, suffering the embarrassment of their linen indecency.

CHAPTER V

With a near-silent laugh on his lips, Axel re-entered Tobias' hut. As soon as he was inside, he guffawed loudly, plunking himself down in the armchair. Though it was plushy, he could still feel the wood of the frame beneath the feather pillows.

Meredith was once again on the floor, poring over her books. Her eyes scanned the pages so quickly that she almost didn't appear to be reading, and she had a strand of hair in her mouth, chewing. Axel raised his eyebrow at her for only a moment before brushing aside the odd habit.

"What have you done now, boy?" Tobias' gruff voice came from the hall. He was leaning in the doorframe, trying to look angry, but there was a smile on his face, so it failed. Under his eyes, there were thin bags, just on the cusp of dark purple. His hair looked even greyer than the day before.

"I got ma compass, an' at the gate I saw a woman fightin' the guards, but they 'nabbed 'er. Now they're gonna kill 'er, too. I can't le' tha' 'appen 'gain! I a'ready los' ma friends to them fiends! We gotta save 'er!" he said, the words falling so quickly off his tongue that Tobias barely kept up, shown by the confused look on his face as he processed the jumbled mess.

Tobias sighed, pinching the bridge of his nose and shaking his head toward the scuffed floor. "Axel, we can't just go saving people from the guards. We barely got you out of their path – which I still regret, but Meredith was insistent," he added with a low grumble, sending a stern look toward his daughter out of the corner of his eyes. She just grinned up at him cheekily, much more comfortable within her own house than she was out in the busy crowd. "Anyway, by now she'll be in the dungeons. With all their defences, how do you propose we get her out?"

"We'll sneak in. I got the uniforms from the guards she beat up. Just stashed 'em outside." Axel replied.

"Okay…" Tobias said, stuttering in utter confusion. "Then, why should we save her? You don't even know her, and it'll be very dangerous. And not to mention we'll have to sneak in without arousing suspicion, even with the uniforms, we don't know the regular schedule of the guards and they might figure us out. And what if those other guards wake up without they're uniforms? They'll warn the others for sure."

"Firs' of all, it's 'cause I can't just let another person die when I could'a done somethin' ta stop it," Axel replied, his voice earnest. There was a general pain in the tone he used, almost undetected under the false bravado of his vehemence. "And second, don't worry 'bout the guards, we'll figure it out, and 'sides, I dumped 'em in a cart on its way outta town. They won't be back in time ta warn 'em."

Right then and there, Tobias – who prided himself on his ability to read people – saw how much the loss of both of his families was causing the poor boy. "Fine." He ceded, letting a defeated sigh pass his lips. Axel grinned and pushed himself out of the chair, hobbling over to the back door. Opening it, he dragged the heavy uniforms inside and dumped them in the middle of the living room.

"Hey!" Meredith protested as they fell over her book, nearly ripping a page. She seized her book, closing it with a snap as she held it to her chest protectively.

"Sorry," Axel muttered. He dropped them, and the chainmail landed with a loud clatter on the old wooden boards that made up the living room floor. "Anyway, I was thinkin'..."

*

CHAPTER V

Tobias and Axel donned the uniforms, and after much struggle and a few minutes of practicing to walk in the heavy armour – or, rather close onto an hour – they snuck out of the house through the back door. Their chainmail jangled quietly as they ambled down the street, the tiny links shifting constantly from the movement. Then, exiting the alley, they straightened to walk normally, taking the postures that they'd seen the real palace guards using as they patrolled.

It was almost too easy as they tromped straight through the front gate, nodding to the guard on duty and receiving only a nod in return as he allowed them to pass. Their boots were heavy on the wood planks of the drawbridge, but as soon as the metal soles met stone bricks, it was as if a weight was lifted off the interlopers' shoulders. Just like that, they were in the courtyard. Passed only by a quartet of knights on their way out on horseback, Tobias and Axel shuffled forward with as much confidence as they could muster under the stares of everyone around them. There were three sets of guards nearby, each stationed at separate entrances to the main palace. Around them, the patrolling guards were unsuspecting as Tobias and Axel sauntered right up the main stairs and in through the overwhelmingly huge doors of the building.

Only once inside and away from prying eyes, the two disguised renegades relaxed and began to head down to the dungeons. Their first turn was left through a large room, passed another set of stairs – ignoring it –

instead entering a smaller corridor through a narrow doorway to the side.

"This way," Tobias whispered to Axel. The thief looked up at him to see that he was pointing, and they both took a left turn. Around them, the walls were mostly bare, with only the rare tapestry strung up from floor to ceiling.

As they descended the wide, shallow stairs, Axel whispered back, "Straighten up a little, an' don't look nervous. I know we're wearin' helmets, bu' ya still can't look nervous. It's in the way ya walk."

Tobias nodded. "Kind of cold down here, isn't it?" he asked, rubbing his arms. The chill was instantaneous, and it sent shivers down both their spines, despite the many layers of heavy clothing they were wearing. He squinted in the dim light that the torches produced, as the only light in the spiralling stairwell came from them. The walls were damp, and due to only small fires, it was quite dark. Tobias did everything in his power not to slip on one of the patches of moss that flourished in the conditions of the stairs.

"Yeah, I guess." Axel was shivering as well. Then, he looked over at Tobias as they reached the bottom. "Slow down. When yer walking, walk. Don't run," the boy scolded quietly.

"Okay."

CHAPTER V

They came to another pair of guards, this time, the ones guarding the dungeons.

"Let me talk to the guards," the older man said.

Axel made no move to step forward, giving Tobias full rein to grab the guards' attention.

"We're here to visit one of the prisoners. Emperor's orders," Tobias said, making his voice as steady as possible. He knew only one of these men, but he'd been to the man's house, played with his children, ate at his table.And now, here he was, standing stiff and unmoving as a guard with a care for anything, not even his own family, who were most likely worried sick about him.

"Five minutes. In and out," one guard said as they both stepped aside.

"Naturally," Tobias replied as he inclined his head.

He and Axel walked down the row of cells, each room holding a prisoner in similar condition: unconscious, bruised, and bloody. The prisoner they were interested in was no different. She lay, unconscious in the middle of the small cell, tangled hair haloing her face, only bringing out the bruise above her left eye and the cut on her cheek.

"The man who 'it 'er must'a been wearin' a ring. I know the marks," Axel said, thinking about his own cheek, where there was a similarly shaped scar, standing stark white against his tanned skin. Currently, it was covered by the helmet, but Tobias easily inferred the meaning of the boy's words.

Picking the lock with a thin metal pick, Axel unlocked the cell, swinging the door open as quietly as he could. The two men went into the cell and picked up the woman.

"What do we do now?" Axel asked, "We can't exactly mosey past the guards with 'er, now can we?"

Tobias smiled. "You forget, I used to be the architect to the emperor. I know every passage in this palace, including the secret ones that I designed for the previous emperor. Absinthe probably doesn't even know about them," he said, tapping the side of his head.

Axel grinned. "Sweet!"

Instead of going back to where the guards were, Tobias led them to the end of the row of cells, after swinging the woman's cell door closed again. At the end of the hall, it was a dead end. Until that is, Tobias reached under the nearest brazier and pulled a lever, causing the wall to slowly pull itself apart at the bricks. It sank back, then opened to reveal a path for them to walk through. On the way down the tunnel, Axel heard the wall closing and grinned to himself. Their plan was going well. Very well. Just before it slid completely shut, there was a loud shout, making it obvious that the guards knew they escaped with the woman. Her head lolled between them as they carried her, one arm over each of their shoulders, down the dark hallway. It was pitch black as there were no torches, but the echoing of their footsteps told Axel that it was a straight passage, so as long as they kept moving forward, they'd reach the end eventually.

"Good thing I'm not 'fraid of the dark," he jested to Tobias, who chuckled along with him.

"Yeah, good thing."

The two men were quiet again until they saw a sliver of light up ahead, and Tobias ran his hand along the wall, found another switch, and the wall opened in a similar fashion as the last one, this time revealing stairs up to a circular chamber.

"Where are we?" Axel asked.

"We're inside the fountain," Tobias replied. "The only problem is that we have to sneak out, making sure that no one sees us with this prisoner, and that's going to be difficult."

"All we need is a good distraction," Axel pointed out. "Leave it to me." He grabbed a reasonably sized stone from the ground and went over to the door that Tobias pointed out. Then, stepping out halfway, he threw the stone at the booth with the fruit.

There was a splat, then a scream, then a barrage of yelling took over, and soon, the entire marketplace was rolling again, everyone pushing to see what was going on.

"Come on!" Axel said, "We won't 'ave much time now!"

They darted out of the fountain together, the woman still between them, and minutes later were in the shadows of the alley behind Tobias' hut. Meredith opened the door, ushering them inside.

"What took you so long?" she demanded as they followed her through the house into the spare bedroom where Axel had slept the night before. The men set her down on the bed, as per Meredith's instructions.

"Never mind," she said suddenly. "Shoo! Let me do my work. You can stay in the living room until I'm done."

Needless to say, the two men found themselves in the living room, both sitting on the floor because neither wanted to be rude and take the chair. Axel sat with one leg tucked under his and the other stretched out, still injured but healing well after Tobias had cleaned it. Axel flexed his injured leg a little with a grin.

"I guess the knife missed all my important bits," he remarked with a smirk.

"Guess so," Tobias said. "Here, let me look at it."

Axel swivelled around, stretching his leg out for the older man to see. Unwrapping the bandages, Tobias rotated his leg and inspected the wound. It would leave a wide scar, but overall, it was healing nicely. "We should give it another wash before you go to sleep tonight," he said, "But otherwise, it's doing well. It should heal fully within the next month or so."

Axel nodded, and once his leg was rewrapped, the two of them descended into silence. They sat there, the quiet around them acting like a cushion to the outside world. Though, despite the calm, there was suspense building in the air between them, thicker than ever. It wasn't physical, but somehow, the heaviness in the air made it harder for both men to breathe. Finally, Tobias spoke, breaking the silence.

"That woman, did you notice what she was wearing?"

"Yeah," Axel replied, "A knife belt, an' a sword 'olster. But there ain't any sharp things in 'em."

"The guards must've disarmed her. My point is, how much do you know about this woman? How do you know she won't just try to kill us, too?"

"I know so 'cause she wants the emperor gone. That gives us somethin' in common," Axel voiced matter-of-factly.

"You do know that in saving her, we've raised the alarm at the palace. As soon as she wakes up, we know she'll either help us or leave, but we also need to go. Saving you was a stretch, but saving her, we can't take the risk. We'll have to flee the city," Tobias pointed out.

"Yeah, sorry 'bout tha'. I didn't mean to ruin yer life," Axel replied, looking down. "I just..."

It's alright, son," Tobias said, resting a hand on the boy's shoulder, "It's about time I did something about the emperor and the rule he has over this kingdom."

With perfect timing, Meredith came out of the spare room with a bright smile on her face. "You can come in now; she's decent."

Almost immediately, the two men jumped to their feet and almost darted into the room to see the woman, still unconscious, but freshly bandaged and in some more comfortable-looking clothes. Her black uniform, both stained with blood, were hanging on the clothing rack in the room, and Meredith had decided to dress her in a white linen shirt and baggy tan-coloured pants from her father's closet.

"Good work, dear," Tobias said, inspecting his daughter's handiwork. "Now all we have to do is wait for her to wake and we can explain the situation to her."

The three of them stood around the bed, staring down at her as they waited for her to wake up and they could finally meet the person they saved.

*

"What?" The voice was one of outrage. "What do you mean she's gone? Did she just up and fly away?" The emperor stomped toward his head of security, a man who, despite his wide shoulders and the scars marring his face, cowered.

48

CHAPTER V

"Please, sir," he said, feebly. "They came in disguise, no one made any alert and when they escaped, they used secrets tunnels that not even I-"

"I do not care!" Absinthe snarled, barring his teeth at the man. Stalking back toward his desk, he swung his arm across its surface, knocking everything down with a resounding crash!

His guards winced, and the grovelling head of security shuffled forward. "Sir…?"

"Leave me! Find this woman and kill her – and anyone else who tries to hide her! I will have their heads for defying me!"

When the man didn't move, Absinthe turned, his long purple cloak whipping around him. "I said go!"

His guard didn't hesitate a second time. He scurried out of the office, quickly followed by the two guards at the door, and they left their emperor to sulk. After they were gone, Absinthe collapsed into his chair, bringing his hands together in front of his chin. His next course of action would have to be calculated and precise. He could not allow for another escape to happen. He knew who she was, of course. Stories of her work circulated the shadier aspects of his kingdom. She was an assassin, here to kill him no doubt. However, it didn't matter who the woman or her accomplices were. All that mattered was that they'd escaped, right from under his nose.

CHAPTER VI

Waking up without appearing conscious was one of the first skills that Ava had mastered during her training.

As an orphan, she didn't have much choice at life, so when a stranger came along, offering her young, seven-year-old self a place to stay, she went along with him and entered the program. There, she trained, and feigning sleep was an ability that she'd learned, its importance up at the top along with hand-to-hand combat and espionage.

That was why when she became aware, she didn't open her eyes right away, her eyes didn't flutter, and a groan didn't escape her lips. She could hear, smell and touch, and those three senses were more confusing than anything else.

In the split second, before she'd fallen unconscious, she'd envisioned what would happen. She expected to

CHAPTER VI

wake up in the dark cell that the guards were sure to bring her to. She expected to be injured and left to bleed out, to die, and if not during the night, to be executed in the morning.

This wasn't the case because she was on a soft surface – a bed, she inferred. The clothes on her were loose and baggy, obviously not hers, and the familiar weight of her weapons in their holsters was gone. She also felt the coarseness of gauze wrapped around her head, her arm, and her ribs, the strong smell of disinfectant and blood filled her nose. The stench alone would've made her cringe, if not for her being used to it for years already.

Then, her hearing came back, and what she heard was the final straw of confusing factors: "Good work, dear. Now, all we have to do is wait for her to wake and we can explain the situation to her."

It was a man's voice; she could tell by the deepness of the tone and the gruffness of it that he was in his mid-forties at least and would probably be greying around the temples already. She also heard three different breathing patterns. One was quiet, one was gruff, and one was faster than the others. Three assailants, she determined. One old man, a young girl, and another young person, but she couldn't pinpoint anything more about the third. If she pretended to just wake up, she'd have the advantage.

Slowly, she let her eyes flutter open and took a deep breath before allowing her breathing to speed up. Seconds later, she opened her eyes fully, scanning her surroundings. It was brighter than she thought and much simpler than what she was expecting. As soon as her eyes landed on the three figures around the bed in which she was laying, she jumped up and tried to attack, but found a strong hand wrapped around her upper arm before she was even on her feet.

The old man that had spoken before had a hold on both of her forearms, keeping her down on the bed as the third person, who she learned was a young boy, moved forward as well to help. She struggled against both men, but with each movement, there was a sharp pain in her ribs, and despite herself, she yelped.

"Oi! Calm down!" the teen boy shouted in her ear, "We're tryin' ta help ya!"

Ava paused, considering her options. She knew by the pain in her ribs that a few of them were broken, or at the very least, cracked. Listening to what they had to say seemed like the best option. As she weighed her options, listening seemed more and more appealing, because...what else could she do? Fight her way out? The choice seemed to have been already made for her.

First, she relaxed, and gave the two males a look. As soon as their grips loosened, she pulled her arms from them, crossed them and remained silent, staring at the teen boy expectantly. Though on the outside she was calm, within, her emotions swirled, heavily dominated by suspicion. Already, five separate escape plans had run their course through her head, but she had to dismiss three of them, due to her injuries hindering her usual limits.

"I saw ya yesterday, fightin' the guards. If yer here to get rid of the emperor, we are, too, so I convinced these nuts to help me spring ya from the dungeons," he explained, gesturing to the other two in the room: the middle-aged man and the young teen girl. He turned back to look at her. "So, will ya help us take 'im down?" he asked.

"Sure," she said with a nod. She could always ditch them on their quest as soon as she was in the clear. "My name is Ava, by the way."

The boy grinned. "I'm Axel. This is Tobias," he pointed to the man, "And this is his daughter, Meredith," he pointed to the girl.

"What do you have against the emperor?" Meredith asked quietly.

"Nothing," Ava admitted, "I'm an assassin and I was hired by an unnamed client to kill him. I just ran into some...complications."

Suddenly, there was a banging on the door. "Open up! We know you're harbouring the prisoner!" a loud voice called through the front door. It echoed throughout the house, reaching everyone in the spare room.

"Oh no! They've found us!" Meredith cried, her voice barely above a whisper, but cracked slightly with panic.

"Quick! This way!" Axel told them and ran out of the room toward the back door. He was barely out of the spare room before they heard more banging on the back door.

"What are we going to do?" Ava asked, trying to sit up on the bed again, but winced and clutched her torso.

"When I quit working at the castle, I anticipated something like this happening," Tobias said, "Come on." He walked around to the far side of the bed and knelt on the floor, shoving the rug out of the way. Underneath, there was a light outline of a trapdoor. Opening it, he propped it open with a metal rod.

"You first Axel, Then Ava and then Meredith so that Ava had support on both sides because of her fractured ribs. I'll follow close behind." He ushered them down the hole, where a ladder was propped against the side of it.

Axel quickly shimmied down the ladder and jumped down to the ground below. His bare feet hit a shallow puddle, sending a small splash around him. Immediately, he was soaked from the ankles down. When he landed, he stumbled a little because of the jolt sent up his leg due to the stab wound. Mud squished up between his toes.

Above him, Ava struggled to climb down; she kept pausing to curl around her middle, holding back a grimace. She groaned as she stepped down in the mud next to him, and Axel immediately steadied her. Then, Meredith splashed down after them and after her came Tobias.

"Alright," said Tobias, "I covered our trail a little, but they'll figure out where we went soon enough. Luckily, the tunnels down here are a maze, so if you stay with me, we can find our way out. Cross your fingers that they don't find us." Putting on a brave face, he couldn't allow the inner turmoil within him to show. For the sake of the other three, he'd have to take charge, and when in charge, there was no room for uncertainty. If only Meredith hadn't seen the poor street boy in their alley and opened the back door to him. They could've just continued with their lives as usual, just like the past fifteen years: without hassle.

He didn't allow himself to reminisce in an impossible future long, so instead of secluding himself within his own mind, Tobias pulled out an unlit torch out of the back pocket of his trousers and struck it against the wall, causing it to light. He held it up, the fire casting a warm glow over the four companions.

"Let's go," Axel said as he stepped aside to let Tobias walk in front of him and lead them on the long trek into the darkness. They began twisting and turning, Tobias leading them past forks in the tunnel with confidence.

"How do you think they found us?" Meredith asked as they passed the fourth fork in the tunnel.

"They must've known Tobias' voice when he talked to 'em," Axel accused.

"It wasn't my dad's fault! Maybe it was you!"

"You did say that they saw us running through the secret passage to the fountain. Also, your stunt with a rock? That was a poor decision," Tobias pointed out.

"An' you had a better idea?" Axel demanded.

The argument continued, three out of four of them accusing the others of them being caught, and then it switched to speculation about what the emperor would do to them once they were found – if they were found.

"He's gonna kill us all. Take our heads right then and there in the courtyard," Axel said flatly. He hoisted Ava a little higher as her arm around his shoulder began to slip.

"I think he'd make an example of us first," Ava voiced.

"Meh. I guess so," the teenager agreed with a half-shrug.

CHAPTER VI

Finally, they made it to an area where a light was glowing from up ahead. They had to squeeze through the last few metres of the tunnel, single file and shuffling sideways to be able to fit. All but Meredith had to suck their guts in to fit. Then, everything stretched out into a wide open plain. In the distance, there was the Nolyss Ridge, reaching into the heavens with its highest peak dressed in a cloak of white powder. The dying glow of the sun was cast over the ridges of the mountain range, bathing the snow-tipped peaks in a warm, peachy glow. Behind them, over the small hill which they had left behind, the city of Arbane stood tall and foreboding in the ever-darkening sky.

"It must be shortly after sunset," Ava said as she tilted her head back to look at the city. Stars were beginning to glow in the navy blue of the sky.

Meredith's head was tilted back as well, her eyes wide as the small, twinkling lights reflected in them, wonder alight on her face. "I see it in my books all the time, and sometimes dad lets me go outside at night to look, but...it's just so magical..." she whispered, in awe of the vast heavens.

"We made it out, but we can't stay here. Surely the guards would see any torch or campfire we light, so we have to keep moving. I say we head west into the mountains. It's our best option. If we travel into the barren lands, they'll be sure to catch us," Tobias suggested as he threw the torch to the ground, stamping it out in the dirt.

"But where can we go?" Axel asked.

"I've heard of a sanctuary on the top of the highest peak of Nolyss Ridge. I've never been there, but I've heard that travellers go there seeking knowledge. Some don't find it, but those who do are left with the answers they were looking for," Ava commented.

"My dad told me 'bout tha', too! Before he…" Axel's voice trailed off, before he spoke again, louder than before. "Anyway, I reckon we'll find out how to beat the emperor up there!" he declared with a matter-of-fact tone of voice.

"We just have to follow that star there, and it will lead us on the best path up the mountain," Ava said, raising an arm weakly to point at a particularly bright patch of stars.

"Follow me!" Meredith said suddenly, turning her face away from the stars for a second, "I can lead the way."

As they began their journey, Axel turned to look at Ava, who was still leaning on his arm, though less than before as she was starting to get used to walking again. "So, how'd ya hear about it?" he received only a shrug in return.

"I get around," she answered. And so, their journey began.

CHAPTER VII

I t was not as fun as one would expect. Typically, the phrase "going on a hike" is harmless. Add in a humongous mountain and the fact that the peak was nestled in its own – most likely freezing – blanket of clouds, harmless was the last word on anyone's mind.

The first part of the climb was relatively easy, with near-flat elevation and a beautifully worn path of pebbles, where the stones were smooth and uniform from the decades of travelers walking upon them and many days and many nights of unholy weather wearing them down.

Upon high moon, they reached their first obstacle. A recent storm must've knocked loose some rocks, or perhaps a large animal up above. Whatever the cause, there had obviously been a rockslide, and their path was blocked by large boulders, all strewn in an uneven heap.

"We can climb them," Ava said, "Just be careful of your leg, Axel." She cast a glance at the bandage – the fourth – and then toward Tobias. "You should help him. He won't be able to walk properly, besides, it's dark, even with the full moon tonight," she commanded in the direction of the older adult.

Though offended by her tone, Tobias nodded, moving to help the younger male to push himself up onto the first stone. They were large, and though rough, had small footholds.

"Ahh!" Meredith cried out suddenly from the front of the group. Her foot must've caught the small fragmented pieces of rock and dust that coated the boulders and slipped out from under her. By some miracle, Ava was at her side, hand gripping the girl's upper arm. She pulled Meredith up again and lowered her so that she sat perched on the rock, though by the grimace that was etched into her face, she regretted the movement as it jolted her ribs.

"I'm sorry!" Meredith whimpered, looking up at Ava. Small tears had gathered in her eyes like liquid silver in the light of the stars as she laid her eyes upon the pain on her saviour's shadowed face. "I'll try not to slip again!"

CHAPTER VII

"No problem, kid," Ava growled, trying in vain to mask her discomfort. "I've had worse, trust me. Just...be careful, okay?"

Meredith nodded. The girl smiled at the assassin once more before she stood and carefully made her way up over the pile of boulders, moving at a turtle's pace, which caused a whole new set of problems, as they were delayed immensely. Though, in hindsight, they were in no hurry and safety always trumped speed.

When the boulders no longer blocked their path, it was once again an easy trek. Though the path did narrow, and more vines crawled along the trail, they walked where many had done so before them, until they were deep into a cluster of trees, causing the moon's glow to disappear from up above and stars to wink one last time before being veiled by increasing foliage.

By the stars, Meredith led them well, but as they pushed deeper into the undergrowth, they lost their path.

"There shouldn't be many more trees, now," Ava said, "I saw from down below that it was only a small patch. Other than this, there weren't any more trees up here."

"Then why'd we come this way?" Axel growled. "Why didn't we skip the trees alt'gether?"

"Because," Ava said sharply, "It's the easiest path up the mountain."

"No' easy if we lose the stinkin' path!"

"Shut up, kid! We're just about out!" she snapped, pushing ahead. Seconds later, she was stumbling out of the shrubbery. Turning, Ava stomped her foot on the loose dirt with a grin of triumph. "See? What did I tell ya?"

Axel avoided her eyes, grumbling under his breath. Eyebrows furrowed, he limped faster, out of Tobias' helping reach and past the smug assassin. "I hate you," he growled as he shoved her aside.

"I know," she replied, though her grin hadn't fallen. She knew that it was all in fun, since the kid obviously didn't like to lose. "But you wanted me here, so you'll have to deal with me until we get to the top of this mountain."

They continued hiking until midday, when their exhaustion seemed to have reached its peak, though theirs was still a long journey ahead and didn't appear to be getting any closer. The weight of their sleepless night shortened their strides and lengthened their breaths until their chests were heaving.

Finally, when the sun was dipping into the horizon, marking their first full day on the run, Ava stopped and sat. "Let's sleep tonight," she suggested. "We're far enough away that our fire won't arouse suspicion. We'll just look like everyday travelers up here." Throughout the day, her pace had grown sluggish, and her eyelids were starting to droop, though she refused to allow them to fall completely.

"Aw…you tired?" Axel teased, though his eyes were drooping as well. "I can las' 'nother night…stayin' 'wake…" He trailed off, voice fading as his tongue stopped functioning.

"No," Ava denied vehemently, her voice powered by stubbornness alone, as it sure wasn't her abundant energy – lack of abundant energy. "I'm thinking of you guys. Obviously, you're not used to staying awake for nights on end."

"No need for the snide comments, thank you, Ava," Tobias said in his ever-polite tone, though it held annoyance for the first time since the journey began.

"Sorry, dad," Ava snarled.

"Hey!" Meredith intervened. "I think we're all just a little tired. Why don't we set up camp and get some rest, just like Ava said, and not fight about it?"

Axel sniffed pointedly, as did Ava, while Tobias gave his daughter a grateful look. He pulled her into a side hug as the other two members of their caravan curled up, making sure to be on opposite sides of the clearing from each other.

"They're going to be a bit of a problem, aren't they?" Meredith asked her father as they also got ready to sleep. She removed her scarf – the only thing that she brought that was remotely close to a pillow and rolled it up to rest her head. Her father, having no scarf, used his arm.

"Yeah," he said with a gentle sigh.

"But Axel asked her to come, didn't he? He was the one who wanted to save her in the first place."

"And you wanted to save him. That doesn't mean we'll all get along perfectly. There's bound to be some conflict; every group has it."

With her father's wise words echoing in her head, Meredith closed her eyes, ready for sleep.

The next morning came in a hurry, almost as if closing her eyes turned on the sun. Before Meredith knew it, she was being shaken awake with bright sunlight in her face.

"The sun hates me," she said with a groan, after giving a hiss and throwing a hand over her face to block the light.

As soon as she was back on her feet, they were back on their path. The hill had gotten steeper from there, though with her excellent leadership, Meredith was able to lead them along what appeared to be a goat trail. It was narrow, sure, but it was better than the sheer cliff just on the other side of the shallow valley between Norlyss' two peaks.

CHAPTER VII

Instead, they had to deal with the bushes that popped up randomly in their path and the weeds that pushed their sprouts up between the rocks, spreading to catch the light. For the most part, it was quiet, because they were all growing tired once again, the single night of sleep amidst their climbing having little effect on their exhaustion.

By the third night, the four travelers neared the top, which had been visible, even from the base of the mountain.

"Look!" Meredith shouted, though she was slightly breathless from the altitude. "We're almost there!" With a shaky hand, she pointed.

"Looks like it, kid," Ava said, "Good work getting us here." Closing her eyes for an extra long blink, she mumbled quietly, "Just a little more now."

Despite the night's sleep she'd had, the strain of the climbing and her injuries were taking their toll. Every step wobbled, her legs constantly threatening to give out beneath her. Because of it, halfway up, Tobias had grabbed her and pulled her arm around his shoulder, seeing as Axel was too stubborn to accept help, and was limping ahead of them, freeing his helping hand.

By the time they reached the top of the mountain, the sun was setting on their third full day outside the city and they were all on the verge of collapsing. Air forced its way in and out of their lungs in ragged gasps, though refused to stay in long enough to give them the supply of oxygen they so desperately needed.

"It's...thin air," Tobias said as he gasped, his lungs desperately clinging to whatever air they could. "It's...completely natural to feel...light-headed up here." His voice was fading.

"All tha'...and...for nothing!" Axel shouted, kicking at the flat rock face at the top of the mountain with his right foot. "Argh! For once...can't something just be...easy?" he demanded.

He and Tobias set Ava down, and the teen plunked himself down on one of the boulders, which promptly began to sink into the ground.

"Ah!" he cried, trying to stand. His arms flailed in useless circles as his balance abandoned him, the stone still sinking further and further into the edge of the cliff until it was completely gone.

"Look!" Meredith said breathlessly, pointing to the flat rock beside them. Or, rather, what was previously a flat rock. Almost in a chain reaction, as soon as the stone disappeared under Axel, the cliff face split open, two large slates pulling themselves apart to reveal an entrance into the mountain. "I guess...that's why it's...called a secret...mountain sanctuary," the teen girl said.

CHAPTER VII

"Well...we might as well...go in," Ava said from where she was sitting. "Can't...just wait out here...for the rest of the...night."

She was helped up again and together, they walked inside, the cliff closing again behind them with a soft grinding of stone against stone. Surprisingly, even as the two slates folded together, it wasn't completely dark inside. Instead, there was a natural glow, like fluorescent moss all around them, filling the hollow centre of the mountain.

Ahead of them, trees and shrubs – life that shouldn't have existed in such an environment – flourished, simply ready to burst with fresh fruit and berries. Ava stared, her eyes wide with disbelief as they cast over the row of apple trees and banana trees and coconuts. There were so many, and they shouldn't have even been able to grow together, much less in a cavern with no way to get direct sunlight, and yet...here they were.

Even stranger – if that was possible – in the exact centre of the mystical garden, there was a temple. It was small but intricate, with columns lining the sides, carved with detailed drawings that were too small for the travellers to make out. On either side of it were two more buildings, each connected to the first by long, sheltered hallways. The roof curved inwards on all three buildings, with the corners raised in subtle points.

In front of the temple, donned in a white robe and whistling a happy tune, was an old man, happily hacking away at the bushes that lined the base of the temple steps. Walking up behind him, the four travellers inhaled deeply, enjoying the fresh air inside, which was surprisingly almost a taste of heaven after the thin, cold air outside on the edge of the cliff that overlooked the eastern valley.

Axel coughed when the man didn't turn but stumbled back as the old man spun suddenly around with a wide grin – as if he'd been expecting them. "Ah! Finally!" he cried, almost impatiently. "You are here! Welcome!"

CHAPTER VIII

"**C**ome! Come! You must see!" the old man declared as he gestured wildly for them to follow before darting off, surprisingly spry for his elderly appearance. His grizzled grey form vanished into the temple, through the doors that remained wide open for them to follow.

The four companions had to run to keep up; Axel was still limping, and Ava was still being supported by Tobias. Meredith was the only one free to keep up, but for her, her short legs kept her alongside the group, trailing behind the stranger.

Once they entered the temple, all that could be heard was the clacking of bare feet on marble, five paces that were varied and all the noises seemed to clamber over one another, as if trying their hardest to be heard.

"Wait up fer a sec'nd, old guy!" Axel called out, panting and swaying as he tried to keep up with the elderly man's brisk pace. It didn't help that the chill of the floor was seeping into his feet and numbing his toes. "Who are ya?"

The man paused and then turned, a confused expression on his face. After a moment of silence, his eyebrows arched in realization, and he smiled brightly. "Oh! Truly sorry, I am! My name is Alfred, and I live up here as the guardian of the eternal library." Then, he gestured again of them to follow him, "Now come! There is much to see!"

The travellers, despite their exhaustion, followed the man further into the temple, past rows upon rows of pews, though all were abandoned. It seemed like the man took great care of the place, though, for there were no cobwebs visible, even though it was unlikely that there were many visitors. Ahead, a shrine stood in the middle, and two hallways were leading in opposite directions to the left and the right.

As the man spoke, Meredith even stifled a yawn. "When I first came here, this place was just a crack in the rock. No trees, no flowers, no fruit. Over time, many travellers have come, and in exchange for the knowledge this library has accumulated, they have shared beauty with me."

He seemed very pleased with himself, so much so that Ava felt the need to congratulate him on his achievement, though refrained herself. She yawned, hers much louder than Meredith's, catching Alfred's attention. "Oh! I see that you have journeyed far. Please, stay the night. I insist on being a good host."

"Thank you very much," Tobias nodded, showing his gratefulness with a gentle smile as he took his daughter's hand with one of his, while still supporting Ava with the other.

The building to the right of the temple was long, with many doors lining the hall, which seemed almost endless until it turned to the left. The doors all looked the same – dark wood, carved with intricate patterns and sporting a golden number on the front in a cursive script. It was almost an illusion to see.

"Each of you will receive your own room, so feel free to choose any of these. I hope you have a good night sleep. In the morning, breakfast will be available across from the temple in the dining room," Alfred said with a pleasant smile, "I wish you wonderful, peaceful dreams tonight."

First, they dropped Ava off, then Tobias escorted Axel to a room and unwrapped his bandage. Surprisingly, there was a medicine cabinet in the room, fully stocked with all the materials he needed for Axel's leg. Before too long, the wound was rewrapped, and Tobias left with his daughter. The two of them stayed in separate rooms that were side by side, just across the hall from the other two.

If Tobias had stayed a little longer, he would have noticed that in the dark, the bandages he's taken from the medical cabinet were glowing a faint gold around Axel's leg.

*

The next morning as promised, Alfred was providing breakfast in the dining room. They all sat together around a large table, well rested and hungry for food. Axel stared ravenously at the food as Alfred spoke in prayer. Not having eaten in the past few days, he was beginning to feel sick to his stomach. Once Alfred finished his prayer, he invited everyone to dig in.

Hands went wild and soon, the fruit on the platters in front of them, once piled high, was scarce. Ava bit into a peach, causing the juice to run all over her fingers. She moaned at the taste as the fruit practically melted in her mouth. She snatched a few more to deposit on her plate for safe keeping.

Tobias, unlike Ava, didn't eat the peaches. He chose to fill his plate with a healthy variety of strawberry jam on a slice of bread, a banana, and a scoop of oats. "I'm impressed with your spread, here," he said after chewing his food slowly, "Do you grow everything yourself?"

The old man nodded. "It gets quite lonely here, so I have my plants to keep me company, I care for them every day, and they provide me with their delicious gifts of sweet fruit, hearty vegetables, and wholesome grains." Then, he stood up with ease, unlike what one would expect from a man of his apparent age. "Now that we're all fed and watered, why don't we continue the tour?"

He led them through the shrine once more, towards the door on the other side, and when he opened it, awe adorned their faces.

The library was the largest building by far and extended both up and down with a multitude of layers, all connected by narrow stairways. Along the walls, bookshelves stood tall and grand, each filled with knowledge.

"As you can see, I have collected a number of volumes over the years. When weary travellers come to my door, they offer tomes or exotic plants as compensation. Their gracious offers are happily accepted in exchange for access to my library."

They walked around the edge of the library, Tobias and Meredith in awe of the rows upon rows of old books lining the shelves, each of which had ten or twenty rows. Axel seemed bored; he wasn't usually interested in books as he'd never learned to read.

"How do you reach the books from the top?" Tobias asked, intrigued.

Alfred chuckled. "When I need one, they come to me," he said mysteriously as he looked back at Tobias out of the corner of his eye.

"If it were up to me, I would just use the ladder," Ava muttered looking pointedly at the wooden device over to their left. She was walking on her own throughout the tour, ribs healed a little more from the rest she'd received – as if some sort of magic was at work – and though she was more interested than Axel, she wasn't as amazed as the other two of their group.

Alfred continued to speak as if Ava hadn't said anything. "I came to live here many years ago, and when I did, it was barely a crack in the mountain. With the help of my prayers and the aid of travellers, it has become what you see before you now, a grand library and safe haven for many." He took a deep breath, inhaling the scent of the old parchment and the stale glue of the bindings.

Finally, Ava interrupted him. "Excuse me, old man; we're grateful and all, but I, for one, have had enough of staring at your collection of tomes. We only came here to ask one question, and I would like to get it and go because the emperor isn't getting any deader while we wait."

Alfred seemed unfazed by her rudeness, "Ask away then, my dear," he said with a twinkle in his eyes.

CHAPTER VIII

Axel had a sneaking suspicion that Alfred had wanted one of them to interrupt. He was probably testing them. It was a test - Axel considered - or the old man was just used to people not caring about his books when they wanted something.

"How do we defeat him? The emperor, I mean. Just point us in the right direction, and we'll read about his magical amulet and be on our way," Ava voiced.

The corners of Alfred's mouth turned up in an amused smile, eyes crinkling as he stared at her for a few seconds of silence before saying, "An excellent question, my dear. It is one that I have been waiting to hear ever since that..." he paused, struggling to find the word. "Since that boy took the throne. I will tell you about it because no matter how long or hard you search, you will not find the information you seek within pages. First, however, I would like you to do something for me."

"What?" she asked.

"I would like you to do something in return. A simple exchange, as many before you have done, and probably many after you as well. What will you provide? I will give you time to think," he said before leaving and shutting the door to the library behind him. The four unlikely companions were left in the entranceway of the library, silence falling over them like a plague, picking their brains for ideas.

"What do we do now? I have nothing to offer him," Meredith muttered.

"Neither do I. Need I remind you that I was stripped of my weapons and then of my clothes before coming here?" Ava questioned, her voice dark.

Meredith blushed. "They were all bloody!" she protested.

"Anyway, we have to find something to do for Alfred, or he won't tell us, no matter how much he wants to, it seems. We cannot be an excuse for what seems to be years of tradition," Tobias spoke up.

"He said that travellers would either bring him books for his library or fruit seeds to add to his garden..." Ava began.

"Wait!" Axel cried out. He began digging through the many patch-work pockets he had, flipping them open and shoving his hands in, only to take them out, empty-handed. "I just remembered... a few days ago, I was pickpocketin' some people in the marketplace-"

"I absolutely love how you're casual about pickpocketing people," Ava cut in, her tone almost dripping with sarcasm.

Axel glared at her. "Says the person who kills people for money! Anyways, I got the pit of a goldfruit in here somewhere!"

CHAPTER VIII

"A goldfruit?" Meredith asked. Her eyes widened sharply in surprise. "Those are so rare! Only lords can afford them!"

"Exactly!" Axel replied impatiently, "Tha's why I need to find it! We can give it to the old man and he'll tell us abou' the emperor!" He shoved his hand into the last pocket, one of the four pockets sewn into the front of his tunic, and declared an "Aha!" as he pulled out a small golden nugget. It almost sparkled in the light, and despite being pure gold, it resembled a peach pit in every way.

"Perfect! Let's go find Alfred and offer it to him. Hopefully, he accepts and tells us what we need to know."

The four of them ran as fast as they could out of the library, which understandably wasn't very fast as Axel and Ava were still injured. They found Alfred in the shrine, sitting in lotus position, meditating. His eyes were closed, face blank and his mouth moving almost unnoticeably as he repeated his mantra.

"Sir, we have decided what we will offer in exchange for the knowledge you possess," Tobias said hesitantly. He wasn't sure what the ethics were for interrupting someone during a state of higher being, but they were in a hurry, and he had said he would be waiting for them.

The old man's eyes snapped open, and the four travellers took a few stuttered steps backward, seeing the white glow emanating from his eyes. Once the glow dimmed, he looked up at them and stood, his gaze curious and expectant. "You have decided?" he asked.

Tobias nodded, turning to Axel with his hand open. The golden seed was passed between them and when it finally came to rest in Alfred's wrinkled palms, he rolled it between his fingers happily. "What a curious object," he mused.

"It's the pit of a goldfruit," Tobias explained as Alfred continued to examine the small golden stone, "Typically, these fruits are only bought and enjoyed by wealthy lords because they are so rare and need very specific conditions to grow, but I am sure that you would be able to give it the love and care it deserves."

"I accept this offering. Please join me in meditation and I will tell you what you need to know."

CHAPTER IX

The five of them sat in a circle around the shrine, the four travellers across from Alfred as they all struggled to copy him in his position.

He sat in lotus, but after watching Axel struggle for several minutes, he switched to a different pose, which was much more manageable for the four others. Once they were all in what Alfred called 'easy pose', he began his story. "If you wish to know the power of the amulets, you must listen carefully to my words, as no such knowledge has ever been written down," Alfred warned.

The other four leaned in, eager to learn more.

"Very well. Close your eyes and focus," he commanded.

They did.

"Your breathing is key. Let the breath fill you, your entire body expanding. Imagine that there is a string on the top of your head, lifting you up and making you weightless."

They did.

"Now exhale, empty the air from your chest, deep from within you. Let every bit of air leave you, allowing new air to fill you once again."

Once again, they did as he described.

"The history of the amulet runs deep in the history of this entire kingdom."

Each of them jumped slightly as bright images flashed behind their eyes. It was a bird's eye view of the entire kingdom, but the mountains had much more snow and the trees were full and vibrant in the forest. "What's happenin'?" Axel demanded. Even though he knew he wasn't really there, he couldn't help but shiver as the cool wind blew past, ruffling his tunic. Ozone filled his nostrils, like stale disinfectant, much like the alcohol that Tobias had soaked his leg in a few days prior.

"As you focus on my voice, I am able to transfer images from my mind to yours. Also scents, sounds, even emotions," Alfred explained, "Just relax and allow it to happen."

Axel relaxed, feeling waves of calm and peace wash over him, though not from within, as he usually experienced. The serenity he felt was forced upon him from an outside influence. He welcomed it.

"There were originally five, each wielded by a master of their craft. Together, they ruled the land, keeping the world in balance. You cannot simply defeat the emperor. His power to control the minds and wills of others is too strong. As he has been using his amulet for many years now, his power has grown."

In their minds, they saw the amulet around the emperor's neck, glowing brightly with black light. Its power surged through their bodies, compressing upon their souls and making their chests constrict. Then, suddenly, it was on the neck of a shadowy figure, looming above them and blocking all light. It was the absence of light itself, giving off no heat, no sound...nothing.

Around this figure, four others stood, each with his own amulet that glowed in a different colour. These, unlike the first, were luminescent, with warmth flowing through their auras.

"Each of the amulets gave its user a different ability, and united, they bring peace and order. To defeat Absinthe, you must find the other four and master their powers as well. You must get them all, for if you don't you shall not be able to remove him from the throne and all will be lost."

The glow of the central amulet brightened, and its dark light consumed them all.

"But even if we already have two, we'll have more than him. Why would we need all four?" Ava asked suspiciously.

"You cannot. The more often an amulet is used, the greater its power becomes. You will never match him in power unless all four of you have an amulet and have mastered its power."

The images stopped and they all opened their eyes. "When the kingdom originally fell many centuries ago, the amulets were hidden away by their previous masters, and acquiring each will test the bravery, determination, wit, and integrity of each of you."

Ava scoffed. "Integrity? What integrity? We're a group of misfits: a thief, an assassin, an ex-architect, and his daughter! How would any of us get past these tests you're talking about?"

"Your pasts are dark, yes, but the tests will challenge you in a different way. If your reasons for seeking these amulets are of pure intensions, I am certain you will find success in your quest."

"Thank you," Meredith said, "Do you know where we might find any of them right now?"

Alfred looked down as they all stood from their meditation positions. "Unfortunately, over the years, I have forgotten where three of them are, but I do know that one is in the hands of the emperor, and I was entrusted with another. I have kept it safe all these years, waiting for you four to claim it, and…" Alfred paused, reaching into the pocket of his robes to retrieve something. He withdrew an amulet, similar to Emperor Absinthe's in style and age, though it glowed with a purity that the emperor's amulet did not. He held it aloft in his hand and closed his eyes.

Axel gave a choked sound. Under him, his feet felt frozen, though at the same time wanted to move forward. His chest constricted, as if trying to fill a gaping hole that had just appeared.

With a smile, Alfred opened his eyes and continued, "And I believe its abilities would most harmonize with you, Axel," he said. He handed it to Axel.

"Thanks," he expressed, admiring it for a second before pulling it over his head. The gem rested against his thin chest, glowing a faint golden colour. Axel's eyes glowed to match it.

Alfred nodded. "It has chosen you. This amulet will now obey your command and yours alone. Upon command, you can become invisible, and with enough practice, that power will extend to anyone you have contact with while using this power." He was frozen for a moment, just smiling at them, before he gave a start, remembering something. "And before you go, you will need supplies, so, with a prayer for your health, I shall gift you with the supplies you will need on your journey."

He quickly darted into the hall where the rooms were and returned a few minutes later with a shoulder sack. Then, the five of them left the temple and began walking toward the entrance of the cavern. Alfred pressed a stone and the wall opened, allowing the bright morning light to shine in from the east, but also allowing in a rush of cold mountaintop air.

"In this bag, you will find four water skins, some provisions, and some firewood. I'm sorry that I cannot provide you with more, but I wish you luck in your quest."

"Where should we head first? Can you point us in the general direction?" Tobias asked.

Pointing to the south, over another ridge of mountains, Alfred said, "When night falls, you will see a star in that direction, brighter than the rest. Just head down the mountain, cross the river and go through the valley. Once you reach the desert, you'll know where to go."

Axel turned to the old man, having suddenly thought of one detail he'd left out. "Hey, old man. How do I use this thing?" He gestured to the amulet, which was glowing pitifully against his dirty tunic. The light flickered.

CHAPTER IX

"When you must to use your ability, simply press a hand against your amulet, and focus on what you wish to do. Even without knowing the ability, if you focus, you will be granted your power."

Axel's eyebrows both raised. "Well, tha' helps," he muttered.

His reaction only drew an amused smile from the old man's lips. "The amulets are powered by strong emotions. The stronger you feel, the more powerful you will become. Be careful, though. It will take practice to master your power. Many years, in fact, but I am sure that with the challenges you will face, by the time you return to face the emperor, you will be ready."

He gave a wink, though Axel was still confused. As it turned out, the wink wasn't meant for him. Instead, it caused the ground to glow beneath their feet with a brilliant white light.

Ava straightened where she was, and suddenly gasped. "My ribs don't hurt anymore!" she exclaimed, pressing her fingers along her torso. Lifting the hem of her shirt, she pulled away the bandages to see that the bruising that had once marred her skin had vanished, leaving only her smooth olive complexion behind. Nothing was there besides a single scar that stretched across her stomach, though it seemed years old already. "How is that even possible?" she asked, looking up as she dropped her shirt to fall back against her skin.

"My sanctuary not only holds knowledge and the gardens that I tend," Alfred said, "They also heal the wounded. You and your young friend here should be in excellent health for the journey to come. Let us just hope it stays that way."

Upon hearing the old man's words, Axel realized that he too was no longer feeling the pain of his wound. He flexed his foot, and the muscles that ran down his leg stretched, as well, without the pain of his injury sending shocks of agony through him. "Tha's amazin', tha' is!" he said with a wide grin stretching across his face. "Good as new, ain't it?" He wiggled his toes as he held up his foot for them all to see, almost losing his balance and falling back on his butt.

With one final goodbye, the four travellers left Alfred at the entrance to his cave and took the first few steps on their journey to stop the emperor from his reign of terror.

CHAPTER X

As the four travellers stepped out into the cold, shivers wracked their bodies. The wind had picked up, more so than it had been on the way up, bringing a northern chill with it. They trekked down the non-existent path once again, but without a star to guide them on the easiest route, they struggled with the more difficult paths. Instead, they followed Meredith's lead down the mountain, as they would when the stars shone in the sky later that night.

"When we ge' to the bottom, we 'ave to cross the river," Axel said as he took cautious steps along the barren rocks and dust, careful not to slip. He spoke between pants, his breath slowly returning to him, but not quick enough to his liking. "How we gonna do tha'?"

"The Malerav River is too deep to wade through, and the current is too strong to swim," Tobias said. "But let's not focus on that right now. We should work on getting down this mountain. Once we reach the river, we'll figure out how to cross it, I'm sure."

Near midday, they finally got to a place of firm footing – a long stretch of flat land almost halfway down the mountain. The way down, surprisingly, had been much easier than the way up, as if they'd been filled with a burst of adrenaline that kept their feet steady and their pace quick. At the flat stretch, the ground was made of soft earth and a cloak of lush green grass, so they correctly assumed that – for the foreseeable hike – it would be an easy trek.

Unfortunately, they were only half right. The ground was still nice for walking, but it wasn't easy. Instead of a peaceful stroll, there was barely any warning as three hooded men jumped down from the tall shade-bearing boulders on either side of them, weapons drawn and aimed at the unsuspecting travellers.

"Don't move, and you! Toss over the bag," one of them demanded, gesturing to Tobias with his jagged-edged sword. The older man tightened his grip on the bag that Alfred had given them – the bag he'd been carrying since the top of the mountain; he wouldn't give it up to a horde of mercenaries. Beside him, he saw Axel reach up to grab a hold of his amulet, closing his eyes to focus. Under his slim fingers, the gem glowed pitifully.

CHAPTER X

After a few seconds, he blinked out of sight, then back in, his body unable to decide whether it was in the real world or not. The mercenaries froze, backing away a few steps.

"What the-" One of them let a stream of curse words slip past his lips as his eyes widened behind his mask. His sword lowered to the ground and his head shot back and forth between Axel's flickering form and the other three people he and his companions were trying to rob.

Once Axel was out of sight for good, the mercenaries were back in action. They tried to attack, but as one ran forward, prepared to strike, he was knocked away from Meredith by an unseen force. The other two stared at the first as he fell back in the dirt with a thud, giving Ava enough of a distraction to take out one of them. She smiled, having waited exactly for that moment to strike.

The second mercenary, however, found Axel and managed to graze him with the blunt edge of his sword with a wild swing, sending the boy sprawling into both the dirt and visibility once more.

Meanwhile, Meredith and Tobias were fending against the first mercenary, who had pushed himself up again and advanced on them while the other two were busy with Ava and Axel. Meredith stuck by her father's side as he wielded a stick that he'd snatched from the ground, using it to fend off the brazen attacks of the more experienced man.

Finally, Ava grabbed the mercenary from behind, holding him in a headlock. "Who sent you?" she demanded.

The man gave a smirk, spitting in the dirt by Tobias' feet. "Wouldn't you like to know?" he asked.

She twisted his arm a little further, causing a scream to erupt from his lips, clawing its way up and out of his throat, but he still refused to answer. Losing her patience, Ava tossed him to the ground, letting him free of her hold. With a firm kick to the head, he was out, just like the other two, whom Ava had also taken care of with the help of Axel.

"What do we do with them?" Meredith asked as she cautiously prodded at one with her foot. It was the one that had been attacking her and her father, who was now sporting a bloody nose but was otherwise unharmed due to his excellent stick-defence.

"I say we just leave 'em here," Axel said. The rest opted to follow his suggestion, so they did just that and returned to walking the rest of the way down the mountain. Soon the ground evened out again, and they were met face to face with the Malerav River – the widest and most well-known river in Ghanara. It fed into Lake Karban and provided life to many people and animals who travelled, as they could easily wade into the shallow inlets along the river's edge and fill their water skins as Axel and Ava were doing for the four of them.

As soon as hers was filled, Ava chugged as much water as she could, her parched throat demanding the cool liquid. It burned like acid on the way down, but afterward, the satisfaction overpowered her discomfort. Looking at the others, she saw that they were doing the same, their pants rolled up to their knees as they waded deeper into the shallow channel that was separated by the actual river by a thin stretch of round stones, exposed by the receding of the river in the summer months.

"It's about lunchtime," Tobias said as he looked up at the sky, shielding his eyes from the midday sun with a single hand and holding his half-empty water skin aloof in his other. Leaving the shallows with refilled pouches, the four of them sat in the shade of the riverside trees and Tobias proportioned out the rations.

"Why don't we get more, dad?" Meredith asked as she stared down at the measly portion.

Tobias gave his daughter an apologetic look. "Sorry, dear, but we don't know when we'll next find food, so we have to make it last."

"Okay..." Meredith replied. She understood, but as she stared down at the portion sizes that each of them had received, her stomach protested. Still, she ate in small bites to make it last, savouring the flavour of the dried fruit, nuts, and oats that Alfred had been so kind to prepare for them.

After lunch, Ava stood and walked away. She stopped in front of a tree, which had lots of smaller branches protruding from its trunk. With a swift roundhouse kick, there was a loud crack as she broke off a branch.

Ava smiled, and grabbed the branch, wielding it like a bo staff as she practiced her moves, spinning around and lashing out with her staff. Her movements were quick, yet controlled, almost like an extension of her arm. Meredith watched, in awe of her companion's true strength.

Meanwhile, Axel practiced as well, though his moves were much different than the assassin's. With his hand constantly touching the jewel on his chest, he ran in tight zigzags, through the trees and along the ledge of the river, jumping over the rocks and fallen trees, though he continued to blink in and out of existence.

"Gotta stay gone..." he mumbled to himself, his teeth clenched and sweat droplets forming on his forehead as the energy of using his ability slowly sapped his strength.

CHAPTER X

He stopped after a full ten minutes, sitting on a rock and dipping his feet in the cool water rushing past. With a sigh, he smiled, and once he was relaxed, he stood and tried again.

Tobias watched the two of them with intent eyes, pondering the extent of their abilities. Axel was an adept thief, sure, but with the new power at his disposal, he would be infinitely useful in their upcoming struggle. And Ava, she was on a level all on her own. Even without an amulet, she was lethal.

Speaking of which, what would be the challenges that Alfred had mentioned? He did express that their journey would be hard, because of course, all worthwhile journeys were, but...it was almost as if he was talking about something else. Something...specifically to do with what they were looking for: the amulets. Would there be guardians for each of the trinkets, like Alfred? Most likely. But what? More people? Or animals instead: creatures of legend?

"Dad let's start packing up."

Tobias looked up, startled out of his thoughts by Meredith's voice. She was standing above him, holding the four waterskins, which were bulging with fresh water from the inlet.

"Good idea, dear," he replied.

Once they were packed up again, Tobias called the other two over. Ava twirled her bo once more and Axel was grinning – though sweaty – because he'd managed to stay invisible for a full ten and a half minutes. The four of them stood together, side by side and stared at the obstacle before them: the river.

On the surface, it seemed like calm waters; easy enough to wade through, but its deceptive appearance hid the true danger beneath the surface. Many an unwise traveller had been swept away by the current, their bodies never found, but stories about them were told as warnings for the next who dared set foot in the water. Only when it reached the gates of Arbane did the current calm, controlled evenly by the grates that barred the river entrance to the city. By the time it passed through the walls, the raging current was tamed and allowed for easy access by the people without any further danger of being taken hostage by its will, the multiple drainage routes made sure of that.

"Ya think the legen'sis true?" Axel asked curiously, his eyes on the water. "Does i' really take people away? I ne'er left Arbane, bu' i' doesn't seem as bad as folks say."

Tobias nodded solemnly.

"It definitely is as bad, maybe worse," Ava replied firmly. "You may not have left the city before, but I've lived along this river most of my life. It's the main route for most of Ghanara because it runs east to west from the coastal plains to the great Lake Karban. I've watched as people stepped into the water despite the warnings and get taken like that." She snapped her fingers for emphasis. "They're dead before they'd reached the lake."

"Then how will we cross?" Meredith asked, her tone getting increasingly worried.

"How does anyone cross a river?" Tobias asked rhetorically, "They use a bridge."

Axel spun around, raising his dark eyebrows at the man suspiciously, but Tobias wasn't looking at him. Rather, the father was looking toward Ava as he spoke, "Before I settled in Arbane with Meredith's mother, I crossed a bridge that ran over the river...west of here? I'm not certain. Is it still there? Do you know it?"

The assassin nodded. "I think it's been improved since you used it, or maybe rebuilt, but there is a bridge west of this spot, if my sense of direction is correct, which it most often is. I crossed it just a few months back," she replied after a moment of thought.

"You can get us there, then?" Axel asked.

Ava shrugged. "Sure. All we have to do is follow the river downstream until we reach the bridge point, then cross, and backtrack until we reach the base of the valley to get through the mountain ridge like Alfred said," she explained nonchalantly. "It'll take us an extra day at most to walk that far, but we're mostly in the shade anyway, and the river will always be close for us to refill our water skins and there are wild berries in this area, if you know which ones aren't poisonous."

"Lead on, then." Axel gestured for her to take the lead, bowing sarcastically.

And thus, they began the estimated day-long trek alongside the river as the sun began to dip lower and lower in the sky in front of them, only blocked out by mountains as Nolyss Ridge curved toward the south.

Their first sight of the bridge was just as the stars began to appear in the sky and the far western points of the horizon changed from brilliant red to darkening indigo. It was rickety in its age, as it was only a rope bridge crossing the two points over the raging white rapids, but it seemed sturdy enough not to creak in the sudden bursts of wind that were channelled through the canyon. They crossed in a single file line, and the bridge held all of them as they travelled the twenty or so metres across the gorge.

Upon reaching the other side, Axel plopped himself onto a rock. "I want to stop for the night," he said.

"No," Ava protested, "We should keep travelling throughout the night. It's cooler and it would cut our time in half. Also, we'll be able to follow the stars without having to wait until tomorrow night."

Axel sighed dramatically and leaned back over the rock until his body was in a near-perfect arch, then he sprang back up quickly, the momentum sending him to

CHAPTER X

his feet. "Fine!" he grumbled, so they began to move southeast, this time, heading upstream and angling toward where the valley would open for them to travel through.

As they reached the mouth of the valley that Alfred had indicated, the silver crescent moon drew to its peak, and they turned to face directly south through the two steep mountains on either side, mountains that almost looked like they had been one, chopped in half by the blow of an axe from the gods.

CHAPTER XI

Facing directly south was a plus for viewing the constellation they were following. It was almost perfectly aligned in the centre of the valley, like an ornament that was specially made to hang above it. True to Alfred's word, the stars in that constellation were far brighter in the sky than any of the others and formed an elegant curve with a long hook curling to both the left and right at the top of it.

Soon enough, the mountains on either side fell away to reveal a wide open plain. The Windra Plains, if they were to ask Ava, named for its uncanny ability to harness the breeze and funnel it toward the Uvian desert, which lay directly south of it.

"There's the desert," Ava said, pointing ahead of them.

"Where? I ain'tseein' no desert!" Axel complained as he squinted into the dark horizon.

CHAPTER XI

"You see that hill over there?" Ava asked as she gestured to a reasonably sized dark mass in the distance, "And how the land falls away after it?"

Axel nodded though it was hard to see in the dark, "Uh huh," he replied.

"The desert is sunken. I think at one point it was a sea, but in a drought, it dried up completely and never came back, like Karban next to it. There's no way to tell, though, because as far as I know, it's always been that way," she explained.

"Alfred said that when we reached the desert, we'd know where to go, right? How exactly do you think that's going to happen?" Tobias queried.

Ava shrugged. "I guess we'll know when we get there."

"So ya trust the old guy?" Axel wanted to know, his eyes falling over her dark silhouette as they walked.

"Yeah, maybe," she stated, "He seemed to know what he was doing." Suddenly, she let out a loud yawn. "I'd say we get to the hill and then make the descent tomorrow," she suggested. "It's getting pretty late."

Tobias and Meredith nodded, causing Axel to toss his arms into the air with a loud sigh. "When I say we rest, ya say 'keep going', but when she does, ya'll go against me!" he whined, "Typical."

The trek across the plains was an uneventful one as Axel was sulking, Ava and Meredith were yawning, and Tobias' eyes were drooping despite his attempts to stay awake.

A gust of wind suddenly cut across the flat land, howling in the sparse trees and the canyons that fed into Nolyss Ridge. Axel shivered as it pulled the hem of his shirt up, allowing the night chill to creep under his clothing and ensnare him in an icy embrace. Ava, to avoid the same problem, hugged her baggy borrowed clothes tighter to her body, the extra layers made by the folds providing a little more warmth. Tobias and Meredith did not face the cold, though, as their clothing, though still thin for the summer, was snugly fitted to their forms and blocked out most of the chill from creeping between the fabric and their bare skin.

As the four of them reached the hill, the sun was just peeking over the eastern horizon, painting the sky in a multitude of vibrant colours ranging from yellow to orange to magenta. It lasted a whole minute and a half before the sky faded into a paler yellow, then eventually to clear blue.

They all but collapsed in the dirt at the base of the hill, just as the land began to slope upward. "Let's stay here a bit," Axel mumbled, his tongue made lazy by his exhaustion. The rest nodded.

CHAPTER XI

"Who will be on first watch?" Tobias asked, "We need someone to keep an eye on us in case bandits or more mercenaries show up."

"I will," Ava volunteered, but her statement was immediately followed by a long yawn, causing Tobias' mouth to stretch into a sympathetic smile.

"It's okay," the father said, "I will take first watch. You all seem tired. Rest, recuperate, and we'll resume our journey in an hour or so. I'll make sure to wake you; does that sound like a plan?"

"Sure," Axel said, but he was already nodding off, and as soon as he laid his head down on a patch of dry, cracked dirt, he was out.

True to his words, Tobias let them sleep for about an hour and a half before waking them, and though Axel was grumpy, and Meredith was still tired, they continued, walking to the edge of the shallow cliff that led down into the sand-strewn badlands of Ghanara. It was a fairly steep slant, but it wasn't that high, so they could slide down easily, casting up dirt along the walls in large clouds. By the time they reached the bottom, all four of them were dusted head to toe in beige and around them, the dirt they'd kicked up hovered in the air.

Meredith descended into a spasm of coughs, and her fingers scrambled for water to wash it away. Luckily, Tobias appeared by her side to rub circles on her back, and three separate water skins were held in her direction as offerings, though she ended up just drinking from her own.

All around them, the same cliffs rose around the desert, boxing them in one large sand pit. In the distance, there were a few dunes, a few desert shrubs peaking out from the sand, and a strange rock formation, half buried in the sand, but other than that, it was a desolate wasteland.

"Now where do we go?" Meredith asked, her voice a little raw from the coughing.

"Alfred said that we'd know once we got here, but...I don't see anything that screams magic amulet," Ava replied, looking around. Suddenly, the wind picked up again, though instead of a cold, chilly gust, it was hot, and brought with it a swirl of sand.

Tobias took Axel's and his daughter's hands, who in turn grabbed Ava's, and the four of them trekked through the endless, ocean-less beach, braving the sandstorm that arose from the depths like a ghost returning to haunt them. Tobias even had to stop the group for a moment for he and Axel to pull their shirts over their noses and mouths; Ava and Meredith covered their faces similarly, though with scarves instead of their shirts. Tobias had to keep his eyes squinted to block out most of the sand from flying in, but it did little against the irritation that the particles in the air brought.

CHAPTER XI

Finally, the architect pulled them under the cover of the rock formation, which, even though it was half buried, provided shelter from the pitiless wind. Together, huddled against the flat face of the formation, Tobias built a fire with the twigs from Alfred's pack and lit it by striking a stone against the rock face.

Though it was midday, the sand had formed clouds around them, blocking the sun from view but doing nothing to keep the summer rays from baking the crisp land below. In the shadow of the formation, it was slightly cooler, but not by much, so they stayed far enough away from the fire not to be overheated, but enough to see each other and not let it be smothered by the sand and the wind.

"Let's just... rest here... and continue searching... when the storm dies down..." Tobias suggested, his words separated by coughs and muffled by his shirt, but mostly understood by his companions as they all nodded back to him, weariness clear on their faces despite being half-hidden.

Tobias got comfortable around the fire, as did they all, taking one last sip from his waterskin. His belly was empty, but his thirst was quenched, and so he was able to fall asleep without much difficulty, especially since he hadn't gotten any sleep since Alfred's mountain.

CHAPTER XII

In the morning, Meredith's eyes were glued together by gritty sand specs and tears, but she managed to force them open.

It was just enough to see that the sandstorm had long since subsided, leaving the desert calm once again, but darkened by shadows in the dull morning light. Because of the lower elevation, the sun's light wouldn't reach it until later, which brought a smile to the young astronomer's face.

She didn't often see the sun, mostly staying inside during the day to read star charts and old books, only venturing outside the safe walls of her father's hut when the night sky was alight with stars and the silver moon. However, her habits did not sit well with her father and he often tried to force her to go out and play in the sun, even going as far as dragging her along on his errands into the marketplace.

CHAPTER XII

Sitting up, Meredith pulled her scarf down from around her mouth and nose, taking in a breath of fresh air. Sighing happily, she rubbed her eyes, trying to clear them of the small particles of sand that clung to her lashes.

Turning her head to look up at the strange rock formation that had sheltered them, prepared to send her prayers to the heavens to whichever god led them there, instead, her jaw dropped. "Everyone! Wake up! You must see this!" she exclaimed, unable to do anything but stare.

Ava was the first to jump to her feet, arms raised in a defensive maneuver. When she saw that it was only Meredith, she calmed, letting out a sigh. "Meredith, this better be-" Then she saw it, and her words faded. "I guess this is what Alfred meant when he told us that we'd know where to go," she muttered, her voice light in her disbelief as if speaking more than a whisper would break the trance that she surely must have been in. "He didn't need to be all mysterious about it, though," she added softly as an afterthought.

"Wha' do ya mean?" Axel asked as he finally began to move, first stretching out his arms and cracking his back before rubbing his eyes. Opening them, the bright green of his irises moved to focus on the two women of the party, but once he saw that they were looking at something, he turned to see what exactly was so interesting. His eyes widened. "Oh."

In front of them, where there'd been nothing but a sand dune surrounding the strange rock formation of their camp, was an opening. It appeared to lead them directly to the centre of the earth. The darkness within made it impossible to see more than a few feet, and the cave barred its jaws mockingly as if daring them to enter.

"This 'as gotta be the place!" Axel exclaimed as he leapt to his feet. "Toby, ligh' a torch an' follow me!" Then, the teenager was off like a shot, his gangly figure somehow carrying him into the darkness at a speed that seemed too fast for a boy his age to be moving.

As he lit the torch, Tobias grumbled. "I always thought teenagers were more sombre than this. Either I've been wrong my entire life, or that boy needs to get his head checked by a physician when we find one."

They walked for a while once they caught up with Axel, who was waiting just beyond the darkness, but after only about fifteen minutes of the twisting tunnels and forks in the road, they were helplessly lost. Stopping in what seemed to be the fifth crossroads where the tunnel split into three, Axel stomped his foot.

"This is 'opeless! We're never going ta find the amule' in 'ere!" he cried loudly. The amulet around his neck grew brighter, its golden glow illuminating the underside of his face like it was expressing its agreement with his statement.

CHAPTER XII

As if answering his frustrated scream, a gust of warm wind – almost like the entire cave was taking a deep breath – swept past them, extinguishing the torch and plunging them into pitch blackness.

"Ahh!" Axel screamed, and by the abrupt thunder of footsteps, the others knew he'd taken off running. He didn't get far, as there was also a loud thump, then a clatter of limbs hitting the ground, then a low groan from up ahead.

"You okay?" Ava called. Her eyes were wide, trying to see anything in the darkness, but until her eyes adjusted, she could see nothing.

"Meh..." a voice replied. It echoed a little in the cave

"Guys, look!" Meredith exclaimed.

"What are we looking at, dear? It's pitch dark in here," Tobias asked as he struggled to relight the torch. The spark just didn't seem to want to ignite. Striking it repeatedly against the side of the tunnel, Tobias growled, then threw the torch to the ground, where it clattered loudly.

"The floor is glowing!" she explained further, and as their eyes adjusted, Ava and Tobias could see it, too. There was a strange, liquid-like substance staining the floor and glowing in a bright greenish-yellow neon.

"Do you think it leads to the right path?" Ava asked.

Tobias, now just barely able to make out her silhouette, shrugged. "I'd hope so because it's all we have to go on."

Following it deeper into the cave, they eventually caught up with Axel, who, after his brief panic-run, was on the ground with a bloody nose and a few scrapes along his cheeks. Tobias hauled him up from the ground where he was sitting and shook him a little to help refocus his brain. All it seemed to do was make Axel's head wobble back and forth, with the sound of a stuttering toad. "You okay, son?" he asked, only to receive an airy nod, but no eye contact.

As they followed the trail, it led them down the steeper paths, the entire cave angling into the depths of the earth. At their first crossroads, they knew where to go, but by the second, the glowing had vanished. The fork in the road had three prongs, each identical in the darkness.

"Which way to do we go?" Meredith asked worriedly. She knew that if she tried to pick a path, she'd panic and pick the wrong one, sending them lost forever into the depths of the strange desert cave, deep below the surface of the earth. The very thought of such a big decision made her feel like hyperventilating.

"This way," both Ava and Axel said at the same time, pointing in opposite directions. Upon noticing each other in the dim light of the still glowing path behind them, they turned to face one another, glaring.

CHAPTER XII

"No! This way!" they said again, in sync for the second time.

Meredith looked to her father, wondering why he was being so quiet, as he'd usually have stepped in by now. All her life, she'd known him to be a pacifist, but the past week had proven that there was a side to her father that she'd never known. Maybe it was the side of him that her mother had known and...loved?

Meredith's heart clenched at the thought of her mother. Tobias often described her as "sweet Maria", the love of his life, and every time she was mentioned, Meredith felt guilt eat away at her heart. It was her fault that her mother was dead. Her fault...

"Let's go this way."

Meredith's vision focused, seeing her father standing at the entrance of the left cavern.

"Why tha' way?" Axel glared, because the left path was Ava's choice. He elbowed the woman in question as she let out a smug breath, though the expression on her face was mostly shadowed by the dim lighting.

"Because I see more of the strange glow up ahead in this direction, which the other two paths lack," Tobias explained, walking down the path without even waiting to see if the others were following.

Two more crossroads met them, chosen by Tobias, who hadn't led them wrong yet. Well, until they were met with the sheer drop into darkness. Axel had almost walked off the edge, his left foot falling into the abyss and the rest of his body starting to follow until Ava grabbed the collar of his tunic from the back.

"Watch it!" she snarled at him as she threw him to the solid ground behind her.

"Well, sorry!" he replied, standing and brushing himself off.

"What do we do now?" Meredith asked. She was slightly farther up the path, away from the ledge, and was slowly shuffling backward since Axel's most recent near-death experience. The other two turned to Tobias.

"We turn back and go the other way. Clearly, this was the wrong path. I apologize." His voice was calm, but Meredith, who'd long since learned to read him, could hear the guilt in his tone. He felt responsible – most likely because he was the oldest, Meredith presumed – and it would take a while for him to forget about what happened because of him.

On the way back up the path, back toward their most recent intersection, she sidled up alongside her father. "It's not your fault," she whispered, taking his calloused hand in her small, smooth one.

"Isn't it?" he asked in reply. "I led them this way. If Ava hadn't grabbed him, Axel's death would have been because of me."

"Well..." Meredith said, "Then let's be glad that Ava grabbed him. Besides, the jerk was bound to fall some time. He's clumsy in the dark because he's scared. It's not your fault that he's scared of the dark, is it?"

"No…" her father replied slowly, trying to work out where she was going with her point.

"Then it's not your fault if he falls in a dark cave because of that fear, by that logic," she iterated. "Therefore, his fall just now wasn't your fault, and all you have to do I lead us the other way and everything will be fine."

Tobias frowned, slightly confuse by his daughter's words, but he sighed anyway, knowing that it would be useless to argue her point. "Okay." He wrapped his arm around her side, starting to feel the chill of the deep earth around them. It was earth that had never seen the light of day, never been warmed by the sun, and therefore was as close to ice as it got in the desert.

By the time Tobias was shivering from the damp icy air, deep below the surface, where the desert is scorched, the cave had opened into a wider cavern, leading in only one other direction which held a faint golden glow from around the corner when it twisted to the left.

Axel, always a thief, snuck ahead at the prospect of treasure, and was delighted by the sight of an entire trove, piled high with gold coins, goblets, and plates so shiny that their reflections were perfectly clear. "Wow!" the boy cried out, a look of pure glee on his face, marred only by the blood that dribbled from his nose. "We hit the jackpot!"

The other three followed him in, standing by the entrance as they watch the young thief standing just slightly ahead of them, frozen by the glorious sight of gold.

"There it is!" Meredith cried, her sharp eyes easily spotting the amulet across the room, glowing faintly blue as it sat amid golden coins. "Alfred was right!" She pointed it out for the others to see.

However, before any of them could make a move to grab it, another hot wind swept against their backs. The wind was followed by the sound of heavy clicking, like a stone tapping on stone. It was an even beat, and it was getting closer.

Turning around, the four weary travellers were met face to face with the glowing red eye of a large golden dragon, who stared down at them with malice.

CHAPTER XIII

With a thundering roar, the dragon stomped its front foot, raising its head.

Dipping its neck and levelling its head, the dragon blew a short burst of fire their way. The flames filled the enclosed space quickly, burning a bright yellowish flame – not too hot but still able to send fear spiralling through them. Like a ravenous beast, the flame ate away at the empty air, greedily sucking away the oxygen.

Tobias and Meredith jumped back, their feet faltering, but Ava – in a reckless move – charged directly at the beast. Compared to it, she was a mouse to a cat, but that didn't stop her as she spun around it, causing the dragon to swivel its long neck around. In doing so, a long stream of sand poured from between its scales, the grinding of the sand against its reptilian armour making a dry hiss that echoed throughout the chamber. The intricate golden plates that layered along its body shone in the light of the flames, reflecting the flickering blaze as it died with a lack of fuel.

As she ran, Ava seized a sparkling sword from its perch in the treasure and swiped it at the dragon's hind end. The blade struck, though bounced uselessly off the thick armour. Despite the lack of pain, the dragon let out a cry that echoed through the cavern, nearly shattering Ava's eardrums as the beast spun toward her. Its whole body rotated slowly in the small space, each step precise and calculated to not step on any of its treasure. Though the dragon seemed too large for its den, it easily maneuvered and once it stopped moving, it had Ava trapped against the wall.

"Hey!" Meredith yelled as she, too, grabbed a sword and struck at the beast, trying to pull its attention away from her newfound friend.

The dragon snarled, and turned again, its tail rolling and its claws clicking against the stone floor. Lowering its head to stare directly at Meredith with one reptilian eye, the dragon blinked, showing off the two sets of eyelids it had – the thick, scaled outer layer, and then a clear inner layer. Its bright, acid-green, slit-pupil eyes remained focused on Meredith for a whole minute before the dragon pulled back, swishing its tail to knock her away and into a pile of gold coins.

Meredith let out a groan but didn't move. Her head rolled to the side, so her cheek was pressed into the coinage, the glittery shine reflecting onto her face and in her eyes.

Then, in defence of his daughter, Tobias darted the to the other side, using the distraction that both Ava and Meredith provided to jump onto the dragon's foreleg and begin to climb up onto its back. He didn't get that far, as the dragon's head whirled around to face him. The long neck that connected its slim head to its snake-like body twisted, muscles rippling beneath the scales, which folded together so perfectly and shifted to allow easy movement as the dragon moved.

With a massive, clawed foot, the dragon tossed him across the chamber, Tobias' body landing solidly on the rock floor beside a large pile of jewels. Just above the jewels was the amulet, and instinctively, Tobias grabbed it and draped it over his head, letting the large blue-glowing gem fall onto his chest.

Immediately, everything in the cave rumbled. The treasure vibrated with energy, trembling as swords, spears, and chalices lifted into the air, shaking off the gold and silver trinkets from around them as they did. An iron sword flew toward Tobias, spinning wildly in the air, and as Meredith saw this she was about to cry out for her father's safety but paused when she saw the blade twist, its hilt landing perfectly in her father's palm. Then, she saw the amulet around his neck, glowing brightly to match his eyes, which illuminated the dark cave as the power of the amulet flowed through him.

Tobias rose, taking slow steps toward the dragon as the beast stood, cowering as its body curled further and further into the corners of the cavern. Lifting the sword into the air, Tobias struck. The dragon flinched.

Nothing happened.

Tobias had buried the sword in the ground, mere feet from the dragon's chest where its heart lay, still beating. Taking its chance, the dragon scurried out of the chamber through another exit and soon, the feathered tip of its tail disappeared into the darkness.

"How'd ya do that?" Axel asked as he reappeared, standing a little closer to the treasure than he had before. As soon as the reptilian beast had appeared, Axel's eyes glowed and he vanished, leaving nothing but a few drops of blood from his nose to prove that he was ever there.

"He got the amulet," Ava said, walking toward the rest of them. In her hand, she held a bejewelled blade that gleamed. She must've picked it up from somewhere in the treasure. "I guess now we know what it does."

As they were about to leave the chamber, there was a jangling. It sounded like coins slipping over one another, so obviously, they all turned back toward Axel. Lo and behold, his pockets were bulging, assumedly full

CHAPTER XIII

of gold. Looking up, Axel faced three disappointed expressions from his companions.

"What?" he asked, "It's not like 'e's gonna miss it."

Sighing, the other three turned away from the thief and kept walking, following the glowing stones back out. The way up was noticeably harder than the way down, as the rocky ground was slippery, and the incline of the path caused Tobias, Meredith, and Axel to slip with every other step.

The chill was back after the dragon had disappeared, seemingly its body warmth was the only thing keeping the chamber down below so cozy. Darkness had surrounded them once again, but with the glow of two amulets lighting the way, they were able to walk smoothly, and it was just dark enough for the glowing substance along their path to shine, leading them along the correct trail.

Back out in the midday desert sun, Meredith took a sip from her waterskin, which was already half-empty. "Now where do we go? It's not like we know where any of the others are," she stated, looking to the others for answers. The next amulet would either be hers or Ava's – she knew that much, and secretly, she wished to receive hers next. She'd already been thinking about what kind of power she'd want, even though it was already quite clear that she wasn't allowed to choose, so it was all just speculation.

Meredith was brought out of her thoughts by her father, who was answering her previous question. Lost in her musings, Meredith almost forgot what her question had been.

"Don't be so sure of that; there's bound to be a way to find the other two," Tobias said. As he spoke, he took a step closer to Axel and was surprised to find that his amulet glowed brighter near Axel's. Then, his amulet lifted on his chest, still glowing, and pointed straight ahead. Staring down at it, he turned, and the amulet shifted in the air to adjust as well, still pointing in the same direction.

Axel checked his compass. "It's pointing east," he announced.

"Then I guess we're going east," Ava said nonchalantly and began walking to the east, which looked the same as the rest of the desert: sand, sand and more sand.

CHAPTER XIV

With two out of four amulets, Ava, Axel, Meredith, and Tobias headed east, but they were running out of water.

Trekking through the desert forced them to take double the sips that they would have otherwise, but still, water was leaving their bodies at a faster rate through their sweat than they were ingesting.

Their only saving grace was the sight in the distance, right at the top of the far cliff's edge. An oasis was shimmering in the desert sun, the bright green leaves of its palm trees lush and healthy.

Axel sped up first, his pockets still jangling with coins as he reached the base of the cliff, jumping up onto the wall to begin the climb. All he managed to do, though, was claw away dirt and inhale particles from the dust cloud of his own making, sending him into a fit of coughs.

Finally, he stopped. "Why - won't – this – work?" he demanded, and with each word, he slammed his fist against the cliff wall that boxed them in the sunken desert. The other three stood behind him, watching as he let his anger and frustration out on the wall until his knuckles were coated in mud – a mix of blood and dirt.

When Axel collapsed from the strain and his dehydration, Tobias took pity on him. "I'm going to try and lift us out," he said, causing the boy's head to shoot up.

"Why didn't ya do tha' earlier?" he cried, his voice cracking. There were tears in his eyes from the desperation that built up in his chest.

"You weren't listening before," Tobias tried to explain, but was interrupted again.

"I don't wanna hear i'! Do i' now!" Axel shouted. He was swaying slightly from exhaustion and all he wanted to do was drink some water, eat some food and sleep under a nice shady tree.

Without a word, Tobias touched the amulet on his chest, causing his eyes to glow for a split second, and suddenly, Axel was lifted into the air. He wobbled slightly in the air as he rose, but within a few minutes, he was at the top where Tobias dropped him in the dirt. Without waiting, Axel sprinted to the oasis and collapsed next to the waterhole that stretched right to the edge of the greenery. By the time the others joined him, his head had been dunked, water running down his back, and he'd taken large gulps from his waterskin, refilling it once or twice until it was full again and sitting next to where he was lying in the shade of a palm tree.

Relaxing by the fresh spring was the best thing that the four of them had experienced since the sanctuary. There were fresh berries growing in the bushes along the spring, and bananas hung in clusters from the trees. In the dirt near the pool, Ava drew a map with the tip of her bejewelled dagger. "We started here, then we went up the mountain and back down to the south," she used her dagger to trace their path over the past couple of days. "Then we went through the desert, so we should be about..." she twirled her knife along the eastern border of the desert. "Here, somewhere. And the next amulet, if we keep going east, should be in this general area." With the tip of the blade, she drew a wide circle around the eastern section of the map, though she stopped at the border where the mountains trailed into flatland and the swamp dried into grass-filled meadows.

"Great. I say we eat now and explore a little more of the oasis. We'll need more supplies once we head out again and find the third amulet," Tobias suggested and was met with nods as everyone stood to head out and collect some food for lunch.

Once they'd all eaten, the four of them explored deeper into the oasis. Ava was in the lead, using her dagger as a machete to hack through the thick shrubbery. The growth of bushes and trees was lush, figs hanging low and ripe next to the bright yellow bananas.

The walked most of the day, and even after they had reached the last banana tree at the far end of the small paradise they'd found, the amulet still pointed east.

"Well, at least now we know that it's not somewhere in the oasis," Meredith said, optimism making her voice a little annoying in Axel's ears. He loathed optimism with a passion, so hearing it about such an important life-or-death scenario was one of his pet peeves. Pulling out his compass, he pretended to study it, eyes fixed on his parents' photograph to avoid having to listening to Meredith's hopeful tone of voice.

As they began to head back to the lagoon in the centre of the oasis, a troop of monkeys suddenly swung by, hooting and hollering and generally making a lot of noise as they passed. One monkey stormed right into Axel, knocking him and his compass to the ground. Upon seeing the shiny object, the monkey snatched it up and ran off with the rest of them, the compass clutched firmly in its fingers.

"No! Come back 'ere! That's mine!" Axel cried, running after it a little before stopping and turning to face the rest of them. "We have'ta ge' it back! Come on! We have'ta catch 'em!" His eyes were wild as he looked at them.

"Why?" Tobias asked, "I mean, I understand that it's a fine piece, but it's just a compass."

"It's no' jus' a compass!" Axel shouted, his anger making his speech even more slurred than usual, "It's the las' thin' my dad gave ta me! It's the las' thin' I got of my parents!" With or without their help, he had to get it back, so he took off without waiting. If they didn't want to help, he didn't need them. He'd never needed anyone before, so he didn't see any reason to start.

Of course, as he ran, Axel didn't see that the other three were also running after him, having made the decision after he'd dashed away, only needing to share a look before darting after him.

In hindsight, chasing after monkeys through a tree rich area was a bad idea. It was nearly impossible to reach them, and by the time the monkeys ran out of trees, they would just switch directions. Finally, the four of them came up with a plan to split up and block the monkeys from getting away. Occasionally, a monkey would split from the pack, but if it wasn't the one holding Axel's compass, easily identified as it clutched the object in one hand and swung with its legs, free arm and tail, they'd let it go.

Axel's body flickered in and out of sight, as he decided that using his power would both help him practice and help him catch the monkey that stole his most prized possession. Tobias did the same with his own power, with one hand on his amulet and the other constantly held in front of his to hone in on the location of the compass. Unfortunately, his grip on the compass wasn't strong enough to pull it from the primate as it fled, but he knew his skills would increase in time.

When they finally cornered the monkey, it was only because the creature had stopped, and turned to them with a cheeky grin on its furry face. Tobias glared at it, panting. Using his ability to manipulate the iron in the object, he yanked the compass out of the primate's fingers. By that time, night had fallen, and the waning moon shone, still bright above them despite its increasingly smaller size, and the sounds of the night creatures scurrying throughout the oasis had reached its peak.

Axel hugged his compass to his chest for the entire trip back to their campsite, murmuring inaudible apologies to it. They sat down around their smouldering fire only to fall asleep with full stomachs and quenched thirsts after stuffing themselves once again. With Tobias' help, the fire was roaring again, providing warmth as they curled up, resting their heads.

CHAPTER XIV

Later that night, Ava was startled awake by a loud scream. Jumping to her feet, she scanned the campsite only to see that Meredith was not where she had fallen asleep earlier. Ava spun around as another scream startled the boys awake, and she saw a sight that horrified her. The young girl was being dragged away by large, burly men wearing all black with dark masks to cover their faces. Immediately shaking the boys to full awareness, though they were still groggy, Ava was quick on her feet as she began to sprint after the bandits in the middle of their kidnapping.

Chasing after the crooks, who had a large advantage of distance, Axel, Tobias, and Ava followed them out of the oasis and through two mountains to the east, into the depths of a rocky, jagged canyon. The walls jutted out on either side of them, making excellent niches for hiding and – in some areas – wide open spaces almost set up specifically for ambushes.

Suddenly, Ava paused, holding her arm out to the side to stop the boys. Not stopping soon enough, Axel barrelled right into Ava's arm, and due to his light, lanky stature, fell back onto his butt in the dirt with a quiet "oof". Behind him, Tobias had stopped in time, and just let out a quiet chuckle at the boy's predicament.

As she leaned around the corner to watch the bandits drag Meredith into a cave up ahead, Ava completely missed the glare that Axel was sending her away from his place on the ground.

"Come on," she whispered, "They were obviously looking for us, and they took her because she's the easiest target. Tobias, stay here, be a lookout for us. Axel and I will be able to sneak in there and save your daughter, but we'll need you to warn us if anyone else shows up. Also, you're our trump card so if anything goes wrong, you can come in and use your amulet to help fight off the bandits."

Both men nodded, but as Axel stood and dusted himself off, he looked apprehensive. "Are you sure I have to go in?" he asked, "There sure are a lot of bandits..."

"Exactly, which is why I'm going to distract them while you sneak in with your invisibility and save Meredith," Ava said as if it were the most obvious thing in the world. "you'll have to leave your gold coins here, though. Can't have you alerting the guards with your jangling."

"What? No!" he protested but was cut off by Tobias.

"I'll keep them safe for you. It's just until my daughter is safe and out of the hands of those bandits. You *can* live without your stolen gold for that long, can't you?" He'd used his "Dad voice", so Axel couldn't argue with that any further.

CHAPTER XIV

Axel emptied his pockets, then touched his amulet, letting his eyes glow for a moment before completely disappearing. "I'm ready," his disembodied voice sounded from nearby. He was already on the move. Luckily, he'd gotten more practice since first receiving it, and was able to stay entirely invisible. Pretty soon, he'd have it mastered. Sort of.

Taking a deep breath, Ava prepared herself for the idiotic thing she was about to do. She turned around the corner of the cliff behind which she was hiding, hugging the shadows. After waiting for two more bandits to come out for their guard exchange, she jumped out, stepping into the light with a loud shout. "Hey! Do any of you know where I can find a medium-sized, fourteen-year-old girl who's been recently kidnapped?"

The guards' heads shot up, all of them just staring for a few seconds, completely and utterly shocked, before they charged.

CHAPTER XV

A ttacking head-on, Ava easily incapacitated two of the guards within a few minutes, her long years of training paying off for once.

Ever since being taken down by the guards at the emperor's palace, she had berated herself for being so stupid in her fighting style that she would allow herself to be captured. If it hadn't been for Axel and Tobias, she'd probably already have been dead for days, and she planned on repaying that debt through taking down the emperor, but first...she'd have to help Meredith be freed from the bandits. Though she would never admit it, Ava had developed a liking for her three travel companions. She didn't typically get attached, but she was sure that if – when – she took off, she'd miss them.

As soon as the first two bandits hit the ground, more bandits flooded out through the cave entrance, at least fifteen more of them ready and prepared to fight. She knew that she would not be able to fight them all, so, breaking tactic, she turned and sprinted her way back down the canyon as fast as she could, hoping that they'd all take the bait and follow her. Luckily – or unluckily, depending on how one looked at it – they did, and she was running with twenty or so bandits on her tail through the narrow canyon, praying to a god that she didn't even believe in that Axel wouldn't be the coward he was like he had been with the dragon.

*

Meanwhile, Axel – still invisible – snuck into the cave as soon as the bandits started to chase after Ava. She hadn't given him any kind of signal, but he figured that it was as good a time as any when most of them were out of the way. He entered the cave, allowing his eyes a second to adjust to the darkness, only illuminated by a few oil lamps that sat on crate-tables. There were still a few bandits left inside, maybe two or three that Axel saw, but he chose not to focus on them as he snuck around, placing his bare feet carefully on the worn-down stone floor.

Around him in the darkness, he saw cots, papers, dirty clothes, but no cage or dungeon. Where could Meredith be? The only place he couldn't see was a small part near the back of the cave, sectioned off with a wide drape of cloth. He began by causing a little grief for the bandits by snatching a few of their things and setting small trip wires for them while they weren't looking. His traps would at least slow them down should he be discovered.

Eventually, he made his way to the back, pushing aside the curtain just so that he could get through, but not so much that the bandits would notice if they were to look over. Once he'd slipped inside, Axel's eyes wandered over the leader's quarters. There was a cot pushed up into the corner. A desk sat in the centre, piled high with papers and documents. Along the wall, there were trophies from his most valued thefts most likely.

None of those interested Axel. He did find a map and a stack of wanted posters of the desk, but he was more focused on the cage that sat to one side, which held a very familiar young lady that he was looking for. Snatching up the map and posters, he stuffed them in his back pocket and went over to the cage, where the girl hadn't even noticed the ruffling of the papers. Axel grinned, happy that he'd found her, though the corners of his mouth fell once he saw the state she was in.

She sat dejectedly in the far reaches of the cage, drawn into herself with her wrists chained – already chafed – and her right eye was bruised, the colour spreading down her face through her nose. Becoming visible, Axel silenced her with a finger to his lips as she cried out in shock at his sudden appearance.

CHAPTER XV

"I'm 'ere ta rescue ya," he explained quietly, before grabbing the lock, studying it. It was an old lock, and he didn't have anything to pick it with, so his eyes scanned the room. Upon seeing a set of keys on the far wall, he scurried over, grabbed it and returned to the cage, trying and testing each key.

"Why's this guy need so many damn keys?" he muttered as he attempted to shove the seventh or so key into the lock, only for it not to work. As he got to the last three keys on the ring, the sound of footsteps approaching entered his ears. There were voices, too, getting louder and louder.

There was no time. If whoever was coming walked in, they'd see Axel and they would both be doomed. Discarding the keys, Axel drew the bejewelled knife that he'd snatched from Ava before sneaking away and raised it in the air. With one powerful downward swing, the dagger cut through the lock as if it were warm butter, the blade glowing with magic. Wrenching the door open, Axel's hand wrapped around Meredith's upper arm, using the other to tap the knife against his amulet, and after a moment of his eyes glowing, they both vanished just as the curtain was drawn back to reveal two burly men dressed in all black.

The two bandits walked in but immediately froze as they saw the empty cage and the state of their lock. In a clatter of footsteps, they dashed to the cage to inspect it, not believing their eyes.

"That girl dis-disa-disapp... she's gone!" one cried, his eyes wide as he stared into the empty space.

As the bandits were wondering where in the world they could be, Axel and Meredith snuck out of the leader's quarters, only to be met with the backs of the other twenty bandits. They were standing all in a row, shoulder to shoulder as they blocked Ava from getting in.

Suddenly, after a moment of the two teens standing frozen – not knowing what to do – Ava appeared through the crowd of bandits, cutting them down with a different blade, one she probably grabbed from a bandit. Behind her was Tobias, who carried a sword, and whose eyes were glowing as he drew the bandits' weapons away. With Axel and Meredith cutting them down from behind, and Ava and Tobias destroying them from within, the bandits were beaten all too soon, grumbling and whining about magic.

As the four met up once again, Tobias made quick work of the handcuffs on his daughter's wrists, and seconds later, they ran out of the cave just as a few more bandits flooded into the main cavern. To cover their escape, Tobias grabbed his amulet, one hand still wrapped around his daughter, and his eyes glowed, causing every weapon from the bandit's camp to cluster together at the entrance of the cave, blocking any chance of escape. They'd surely be able to move everything, but it would give the four of them just enough time to get away and prevent any chance of the bandits from catching up to them.

Their footsteps were the only ones as they ran down the narrow canyon, though it was so twisted that they took the first turn they could, the group turning north and heading back toward Arbane. If they were to go back to the oasis, the bandits would find them again. Luckily, Tobias had grabbed their supplies before taking off after Ava and Axel to rescue Meredith.

CHAPTER XVI

As soon as they were past the first subset of mountains, out of the narrow canyon and into a wider valley, Axel spoke up, startling Meredith out of the traumatic thoughts of her recent kidnapping. Not much had happened, but she was sure that she would never be able to really talk about the experience.

"Hey, I foun' some pretty cool stuff when I got Meredith outta there," the other teen said, digging a hand into the pocket on the back of his trousers. He pulled out a handful of papers, mostly crumpled but still intact. "I can't read, but I know ones a map an' the other had our pictures, so I though' they were 'bout us," he explained as he handed the papers to Meredith, who was closest to him.

Scanning the papers, Meredith determined that Axel was indeed right: one was a map of Ghanara, and the others were...demands of their arrest. She shuffled through the scrolls detailing them, and from over her shoulder, Meredith saw Ava raise an eyebrow at her own.

"Wow," the assassin muttered, "That was quick. No wonder the bandits were after us. Look how much the emperor's offering for our capture."

"How'd they get our pictures?" Meredith asked, staring at the scroll of herself in horror. She looked utterly terrible; the artist made her seem like a bloodthirsty beast from Kyrr, the land down below.

Ava pointed at the map. "Aha! See, I knew I was right. The bandits marked their own headquarters on this thing, what idiots! But they did also mark a temple over here. Must've scouted it and planned an attack or something. It looks like just the right place to find the third amulet. If it's not there, I swear I'll eat my scarf," she said.

"But..." Meredith was confused, "If an amulet is at the temple, wouldn't it have been found already? I mean...the bandits know where it is, and even if it's not marked on the map, if they found it, others must've, too."

"Maybe we need to use the other amulets to get to this one. If someone had found it, we'd have heard about it. Even if it's not there, it's on our way and definitely worth a look," Tobias suggested. Ava nodded along with his statement, as did Axel.

Meredith was still a little skeptical, but finally, she shrugged. "I guess it can't hurt," she said.

"Yeah, if we don' find an amulet there, we'll die sooner or later, 'specially with such high prices on our heads," Axel pointed out, trying to lift the mood, but failing.

"Anyway," Tobias said forcefully, sending Axel a stern look when his daughter's face fell. "If it is there, we'll have a better chance than any to get it, and we'll be one step closer to finding the last one and taking down the emperor."

When they continued walking, Axel snatched the map from Meredith's hands and was holding it in front of him professionally, though he had no idea how to read it. Meredith had to turn it in his hands because it was upside-down, but the other teen said nothing otherwise.

The four of them made a few wrong turns, digging deeper into the thick shrubbery that flourished in the valley. In the underbrush, there was a slight rustling, causing Ava to pause, spinning around to face it.

"There's something out here," she growled in a low voice. Pulling out the dagger she'd acquired, she held it at the ready, eyes sharp and searching.

The others stopped, turning back to face their tense compatriot. Tobias immediately glanced around, skeptical of the foliage, but Axel crossed his arms, crinkling the map between his fingers.

"Yeah, right," he said, "Wha' could possibly be out 'ere?"

Just his luck, a tiger burst from behind some bushes, snarling loudly to announce itself. White teeth were bared from behind shiny black lips, angry froth dripping from them. The creature stood at twice the height of any tiger Ava had seen before, and its beady eyes glowed red with a knowledge that she knew no jungle cat should have. The tiger was no regular beast, that was clear enough.

"You just had to say something, didn't you?" she said, though she didn't risk taking her eyes off the tiger to glare at the teen. Hearing a rustle of parchment, she knew he'd dropped the map in surprise.

"I didn't mean i', I swear!" His usual drawl was high pitched an panicked, steps wary as he shuffled back from their ambusher. The gravel under his feet rattled, causing the tiger's ears to swivel his way.

"Stop moving!" Ava hissed, and the boy smartly froze.

"Then, what do we do?" Meredith asked. She'd slid in closer to her father when the rustling became apparent but hadn't moved from her place since the beast emerged.

"It's not normal – that's for sure – and by now, it would've ripped us to tiny bits-" Meredith let out a frightened gasp, interrupting Ava. She only received a glare from said adult. "As I was saying, this must be a test of magic. To see if we're worthy of the amulets."

"And how'dyage' tha' idea?"

The tiger snarled again, bringing the four's attention back to it once more. Taking a step forward, its claws dug into the dirt, leaving scars in the earth under its paws.

"It's getting ready to charge!" Ava warned, "Get ready to use your powers!"

"Pardon?" Tobias asked. His eyes were focused on the creature. He took a protective stance in front of his daughter, but he saw no way that they could defeat this creature – as Ava thought. He had control over metal, yes, but in the dense forest, there was no metal for him to control. And Axel's powers were even less useful against an opponent with a heightened sense of smell and hearing.

"We don't have to beat it!" Ava said. "We just have to distract it! To get away!"

The beast suddenly leapt at her, and she was seconds away from being mauled if not for her quick reflexes taking her out of the way. Her feet came back into contact with the ground seconds later, several feet from her previous position, with the tiger flying past her, into a tree. It stood, shaking off the obviously growing headache.

"Ha! The cat kissed the tree!" Axel shouted. His eyes only widened as the beast turned its attention to him, and he yelped, jumping straight up in the air to avoid its claws. Grabbing some low hanging vines, the boy thief climbed higher and higher into the tree like a monkey, as agile in the jungle as he was in the city. It was, after all, just a matter of grabbing and swinging and with the light of day surrounding him, he felt courage welling up inside his chest.

The tiger kept leaping at him, swiping its huge paws, each tipped with five, gleaming white daggers of ivory, which cut clean through the smaller branches, sending vine-ridden boughs of wood spiralling through the air around it.

Roaarrrr! Its growl ripped through the air, reverberating through Tobias chest as he stood his ground, studying the tiger. He felt an off sense of calm within him, maybe from his amulet, and somehow...he knew that they would be able to overcome the tiger's relentless attack. If it was indeed sent to test them, then he would do everything in his power to prove himself worthy and save his friends.

With a roar of his own, Tobias pushed his hands forward after briefly brushing his fingertips against the gem, and he felt strength flow through him. The earth shook as tiny particles of metal pushed their way to the surface, responding to his command. Soon, he'd gathered enough to form a thin tornado of metal, and he sent it toward the beast, which had paused in its assault on the boy.

The tiger's ears perked, and it turned just in time to see the oncoming whirlwind. It let out a loud yowl as it was whipped up in the twister. All they could see was a blurred orange splotch as the tiger was raised in the power of the twister, to the very top until it was spit out from the mouth of the tornado and sent flying into the distance.

The howl of its fear was heard, then a loud crash and the crack of breaking branches, then nothing.

"Yay! You did it, dad!" Meredith cried in celebration, jumping into the air and running to tackle her father in a tight hug. She let out a big breath – one she hadn't known she'd been holding – and let relief flood through her.

"How did you do that?" Ava asked, staring wide-eyed at him.

Tobias shrugged.

"You've only had the amulet for a short time. How could you possibly have gotten so good with it already?" she pressed, taking a step closer to him.

Again, Tobias shrugged. "I guess it's like Alfred said. The stronger the emotion, the more powerful the amulet's gift. I just know that I wanted to save you all, and it responded to me," he said.

"Let's keep goin'. Who knows where them bandits is now," Axel suggested. He pulled the map out again. It was even more crinkled, and there were a few rips that weren't there before.

They kept walking, and though Axel was the one who had the map, they followed Meredith, who – with her father at her side – foraged ahead. She stayed quiet, not allowing the thoughts of hopelessness grow, because ever since the dragon, then the bandits, and most recently, a giant tiger, she worried what other challenges lurked in the kingdom she knew so little about.

Instead, it was Ava that protested, when she finally asked, "Why us, though? Why should we be the ones to risk our lives? I mean, there are plenty of others out there, just going through life and complacent to the emperor's rules, regulations, and restrictions, so why should we be the ones to risk our lives for this treasure? I know that we've all been hurt by the emperor, but why should we be the ones that must stop him? We left the city to get away from the guards, sure, but we could have just gone off and lived outside the city, maybe been on the other side of Ghanara by now."

"You know why we have to do this," Meredith replied to both of her travel companions. "The rest of them are sheep, and we have to be the ones to free them from the evil shepherd. He's leading them to their deaths, but if they step out of line to escape, he cracks his staff and they're back on track, unable to resist complying."

"Yeah," Axel agreed, his head snapping up so that he was looking forward, though his words were directed to Ava. "I wan' 'im gone so 'e can't 'urt anyone else e'er again. Ma parents are dead, and now I'm finally gettin' a chance to avenge 'em, so I'm gonna do anythin' to make it 'appen, even if it means I'm gonna die."

"You have issues, kid." Ava grumbled, clearly not enjoying the two of them doubling up against her. "Fine," she said, "But I'm holding the map; you clearly don't know how to read it!" she said to Axel, holding her hand for him to hand it over.

The teen held the map up, out of her reach. "No! I'm holdin' the map! I can lead jus' fine!"

The assassin scowled. She stopped, turning around to face him. "You're so stubborn! Just give it to me! Stop trying to be a man when you're just a kid and let the adult lead!"

"Oi! I was the one ta save ya in the first place! What did you do when the guards gotcha? Nothin'! An' I'm plenty old enough to lead us!" Axel protested, stomping as he walked around her.

CHAPTER XVI

Ava kept walking alongside him, both stomping their feet angrily as if taking their frustration out on the earth would help. Behind them, Tobias and Meredith gave them a wide berth, hoping to stay out of it.

Finally, when Axel gave in and handed over the map, Ava looked at it, gave it a flourish, ready to lead them in the right direction – because clearly Axel had led them astray – but when she looked up, she saw that the temple was just ahead, clearly visible in the distance, just beyond a few trees. She groaned, rolling up the map and using it to slap the top of Axel's head as he grinned childishly at her, sticking out his tongue.

"Come on," she whispered, a scowl marring her usually brilliantly deceiving features. If she couldn't lead them to the temple, she would sure as heck lead them through the temple and prove her worth.

CHAPTER XVII

U pon entering the temple, the two amulets began to glow, both pulsing with an eerie red light. As their glow grew brighter, a red outline appeared on the far wall of the entrance to the temple, above the shrine. Pretty soon, the entire chamber was lit up with the red glow, and Ava, feeling a pull, walked forward.

The wall vanished, revealing a hidden walkway for them.

As they headed through the secret tunnels, it seemed far too quiet. "Is anyone else getting a strange feeling?" Ava whispered, the hairs on the back of her neck beginning to stand on end. Before the others even had the chance to answer, the first trap was sprung.

From the wall, a large axe burst forth, swinging across the corridor.

CHAPTER XVII

"Duck!" Tobias shouted as he tackled his daughter to the floor, knocking her out of the way of the deadly blade. The other two lunged to the ground as well, allowing the blade to swing over their backs, just barely brushing the fabric of their tunics.

After a few more swings, the axe stilled, hanging in the direct centre of the hall behind them. Ava shuffled forward and stood, followed closely by Axel, Tobias, and Meredith. She continued, feeling the pull become stronger than ever. The next trap was a pressure plate on the floor, but Ava stepped over it carefully, the others following her example.

The next trap was a pit, and if anyone asked, Ava would vehemently deny that it was her fault. The floor crumbled beneath their feet, like dry bread. The bottom of the pit – coated with large, sharp spikes – were protruding from the stone bricks below. Ava's heart stopped in her chest, but instincts took over, luckily, and as she fell, her legs spread into the splits, feet catching the sides of two spikes and held her, suspended between them.

"Ava!" she heard Meredith call from above. Looking up, she saw that they were approximately four feet above her.

"I'm fine!" she replied. The muscles in her legs seemed to disagree as they began to shake, straining to hold her as she straddled thin air in a pit of spikes. Well, it can't get much worse from here on out, she thought sarcastically as Tobias' arm lowered into the pit, just enough to grab her own outstretched hand and heave her up.

As soon as she was back on solid ground, Ava let out a breath of relief.

"You okay?" Meredith asked as she kneeled next to her friend.

Ava shoved away the younger female's helping hands and stood on her own, looking ahead of them to see the pit blocking their path. "We'll go around," she said, eyeing the narrow ledge along the side of the crumbled floor.

"Um...you sure it's safe?" Meredith asked hesitantly.

"I'm not turning back now." Pure confidence oozed from Ava's words as she took the first step forward, carefully shuffling her feet along the edge of the wall, her back pressed against the dusty bricks. On the other side, she turned back to the others. "Well? Are you coming, or not?"

With hesitance they followed, shivering in fear the entire way across, especially as grains of the brick fell away and into the pit. "Okay, we're over," Tobias said once all four of them were safely past the trap.

Several more un-tripped trip-wires later, they reached what appeared to be that last room before the final chamber. Unfortunately, from one door, they could only see through the opposite passage to their prize, but in between them and it was a pit of...

"Quicksand," Ava said, staring at the sunken pit with sarcasm obvious in her tone. "Of course, there's quicksand."

Axel shifted to put his weight on his left and his hands rose to his hips as he assessed their newest problem. "Darn. 'ow do we ge' 'cross? Any ideas?"

"I've got nothing," Meredith murmured. "How about you, dad?"

Tobias remained silent for a moment, eyes focused on the quicksand in front of them. He had a look on his face that Meredith knew well: the one where she could almost see his brain moving as he tried his hardest to solve the issue right in front of him. Usually, he got his answer. Their current problem...it wasn't like anything he'd ever seen before. "Nothing. Axel?"

"Nah. Nothin'. I ne'er even seen quicksand b'fore."

"How about you?" Meredith asked, instead looking to Ava.

"Yeah, migh'y leader? Got anythin'? We can't go back now, 'nyway, so yabe'er 'ave a way ferward," Axel called out rudely, though the three of them knew he was joking, as was his unusual sense of humor.

"I've only faced quicksand once before," she said, eyes not leaving the trap. Her voice was quiet as she spoke, ghosts hovering in her eyes as she relived a memory from years prior. "Lost my partner in it. He wasn't smart enough to escape. That's why we called it the Devil's Trap. Because you know you're going to die but cannot escape once you're stuck."

"Then how do we get across? How did you get out?" Meredith pressed. She felt her heart clench at the mention of Ava's previous partner – maybe even a close friend of hers – but they needed to get across. Their mission was set and was just waiting to be fulfilled.

Ava finally looked at her, a grin spread across her features. "We swim, of course," she said, as if it was the most obvious thing in the world. "Throw the bag across. We can't risk carrying it with us as we go." Once the bag was thrown as instructed, the assassin lowered herself onto the quicksand, distributing her weight evenly. Her head rested against the cool, damp surface, and already she felt the grit in her hair, but ignored it.

Sweeping her arms back in wide circles, Ava began to move, slowly and evenly across the sand. Her feet remained still, and about halfway through, she lifted her head slightly to look at her companions.

"See?" she asked, "Easy, right? Just distribute your weight, and once we reach the other side, we can just roll the rest of the way."

CHAPTER XVII

As she said so, she reached the three quarter-way mark, and did just that, turning and rolling the rest of the way until she was back on the hard surface. Standing again, she brushed herself off and shook most of the sandy grime out of her hair.

"Easy."

The other three, like before, were hesitant to follow, but seeing as they had no other option, reluctantly obeyed their leader's command.

Tobias went first. Just as he began to kneel, Ava stopped him. "You'll have to leave Axel's gold coins behind. We can't risk the weight sinking you before you get across."

"Bu'...I worked hard fer those!" Axel protested, "I should get ta keep 'em!"

Ava sighed. "Normally, yes. But not at the expense of someone's life. If we want to all get across and make it out of here alive, we leave the money behind, Axel. Sorry." There seemed to be true sincerity in her voice. As another person who lived from one meal to the next, she knew the struggle of leaving behind money. It seemed like such a lucky break for the boy – she knew the feeling all too well – and asking him to leave it behind...well...she had to remind herself that it was for the sake of a friend.

Axel seemed to understand her point of view as well, because after a moment of Ava conveying her message to him through their locked eyes, the thief sighed. "Alrigh'."

Ava smiled, nodding to Tobias, who'd just finished emptying his pockets of the gold coins that Axel had swiped from the dragon. Laying down as Ava had, he used his strong arms to paddle across on his back, careful to go slow and keep his weight even over the dangerous surface. There was no way to tell how deep it was. It could have been two feet or twenty, but without a long stick to test it, caution was their best friend.

"Okay," he said as he sat on the end near Ava. "I'm here, and I'm alive. Darling?" he called to Meredith, "Your turn now." He smiled reassuringly, gesturing for her to go next.

"Yup…" She gave a nervous giggle. "My turn…" Kneeling, she cautiously ran her hand over the surface of the same, recoiling as the damp particles clung to her skin. A shiver raced through her. With a deep breath, she crossed, though her heart was racing, and her lungs ached from the deep breaths that she refused to take.

Finally, it was Axel's turn.

"Le' me say this now," he began, "I don't wanna do this, bu' I will." Just like the three before him, he lowered himself into the sand, pretending that he was back on the surface of the Uvian desert. Closing his eyes, he imagined the night that they slept under the stars on the mountain, and the feeling of the cool sand under his body from the night of the sandstorm, despite the rough weather around them. He almost relaxed when Ava's shout startled him.

"Start moving! You don't want to stay in one place to long! But...stay calm anyway!" she called loudly, having cupped her hands around her mouth to heighten the sound.

"Thanks fer tha'!" Axel shouted back, slightly annoyed as he opened his eyes to feel that he, indeed, had begun to sink. Quickly moving to begin paddling over, he found that it wasn't as easy as it seemed. First, the sand just swished under his arms, and he didn't even seem to be moving at all – at least not that he noticed.

Also, the sand kept getting in his ears and his hair, making him itch all over, and he was pretty sure that a beetle had crawled in his shirt. Halfway along, though, the real problem happened. At first, it was only a twinge, but then, all at once, Axel froze and curled up, wrapping his hand around his leg.

"Cramp!" he cried, screwing his eyes shut tight as he began to sink, the concentrated weight of his fetal position causing him to sink faster and faster into the depths of the pit.

"Axel! Spread out!" Tobias commanded, desperation filling his voice.

"I can't!" He was half sunken already, the quicksand pooling in his lap.

"You can do it!" Meredith cried.

"No!" the boy denied, "I can't! It hurts so much!" He was almost under within seconds, the sand up to his shoulders and curving around his left ear as he rolled over on his side; the surface was just brushing against the corner of his mouth. Then, with one final gasp and a cough, he was gone, swallowed by the pit.

"Axel!" Meredith cried, launching herself forward only for her father to grab her at the last second, pulling her away from the danger. He pulled her close and she turned to bury her face in his chest, sobbing into his tunic. He'd come to be a close friend, even though he was strange, rude, and loud. In fact, he was the only friend that Meredith ever had. Until...the quicksand ate him. It ate him in one big gulp, like a monster, much more terrifying than the mercenaries, or the tiger, or even the dragon! Her friend could fight against those. He had fought against those, but with the quicksand, he was just...gone.

"Alright, that's it!" Ava shouted, startling the poor, despairing teen. The assassin, without any regard for her own safety, jumped in after him in an impulsive act of bravery - or stupidity. She'd figure that out later.

At first, she was swallowed as well, completely taken into the belly of the beast, but after a few seconds, she surfaced, with Axel right alongside her. Both gasped for large breaths, and as Axel coughed, spitting up sand, Ava righted them both, spreading her weight and shuffling upward to float on the surface of the sand. She'd grabbed him, too, turning him sideways to lay on her stomach. He was still curled in a ball, gagging and coughing.

"You good?" she asked, brushing a hand gently through his hair. Never before had she risked her own life for the sake of another's in such a way, and...it sent a warm feeling through her chest, blooming like a flower. What was that feeling? Ava didn't know, but she sure liked it.

"Yeah..." Axel said between pants of breath, "I'm good..."

Back on the hard surface again, Axel was tempted to kiss the bricks beneath his feet but refrained from doing so as he looked up to see the third amulet on their journey sitting just ahead – past the two open doors mere feet from his face. He stood and walked forward, only to be stopped by Tobias.

"Hey kid," he said, digging into his pocket. "I saved one for you." With a flick, he sent a single golden coin flipping through the air, caught easily by the nimble fingers of the thief. After staring at the golden circle for a moment in disbelief, Axel smiled up at the man.

"Thank you."

The final chamber – as Axel had deemed it in his head – was round, ascending higher and higher the closer to the middle it was. In the direct centre was a pedestal, and perched upon it was the third amulet, with a ruby as the gemstone. It glowed a faint red, responding to the closeness of Axel's and Tobias' amulets.

Ava went to grab it, but as soon as her fingers brushed the gem, the door behind them slammed shut, sealing them within. A thundering crash closely followed the door, and then, near the ceiling of the chamber, two slots slid open, allowing water to flood through them.

They were trapped.

Ava, having snatched the amulet, was about to put it around her neck and discover her power, lost it as Meredith ran over to her in a panic, her flailing arms throwing the amulet onto an empty ledge above their heads. The chain caught on a spire of the brazier, letting the amulet hang dauntingly as if mocking them for their failure.

"Boost me up!" Ava shouted the order, and immediately Tobias was at her side, kneeling to allow her onto his shoulders. Lifting her, he struggled to sustain her weight, his feet shuffling from side to side as he walked her over to the brazier.

CHAPTER XVII

Ava's hand rested on the wall, and she stretched as far as she could to reach the amulet. Her fingers wrapped around the gem, but it was still too high for her to remove from the wall. "A little higher..." she breathed; her voice strained as she stretched, her arm reaching. The tips of her fingers were inches away.

Finally, as Tobias propelled himself onto the tips of his toes, Ava jerked upward, knocking the amulet loose and into her hand. She flung it over her head and around her neck before anything else, and as it glowed on her chest she experienced a strange, floating feeling.

"Whoa!" she heard Axel shout from behind her, prompting her to look down.

Her whole body was shifting in and out of translucency. She wasn't becoming invisible like Axel would; instead, she was almost becoming a ghost. Tobias let her down quickly, staring at her for what seemed like a whole minute before he noticed that the water level was still rising, now around chest-level on Meredith.

"What's her ability?" The young girl questioned, also staring.

Ava had a theory, but first, she'd have to test it. Walking over to a wall, she touched it and focused. When she became translucent, her hand slipped through the stone, disappearing behind the opaque surface. "Intangibility..." she mumbled. She stepped through the wall and was instantly assaulted by bright sunlight. Squinting, she looked around to see that she was at the top of the temple, staring out at the land below.

Quickly darting back in through the wall, she said, "I can get us out of here; come on!" She grabbed Tobias' and Axel's hands, but her translucency only flowed into Axel, Tobias' form flickering pitifully.

She gave a cry of frustration. "Darn it all! I'm not strong enough! I'll have to take you one at a time!" She let go of Tobias and dragged Axel out through the wall. He deserved to be the first out; he'd already had enough near-death experiences for one day. Then, back inside, she grabbed Meredith. By that time, both were floating in the water, kicking and paddling to keep their heads above the surface.

Once Ava and Meredith were through the wall, they dropped down onto the ledge on the outside, splashing Axel. Their clothes were soaked, and when Ava jumped through the wall again, she floundered to the surface to see that Tobias was near the ceiling, in the pitch blackness with only a foot of air left.

"Come on!" she cried, reaching out into the darkness. She couldn't see him well, but she heard the splashing of his flailing hands and the gasps he took as he struggled to keep himself above water. With the added weight of the satchel from Alfred, he was losing energy.

CHAPTER XVII

Grabbing one of his flailing hands, Ava supported the man and paddling them to the wall with a few weak kicks. Focusing all her energy, she pushed through the stone as soon as the chamber filled up, every last bit of air gone.

Outside, they fell a good ten feet before landing with a jarring start to their legs. Tobias collapsed, gasping for air, his hair dripping onto the ground as he blinked droplets out of his eyes.

"Dad!" Meredith cried, running over and dropping to her knees next to him.

"I'm okay, dear. Just need to catch my breath," he replied, waving her off a little. He was panting a little, trying to regain his breath, and he looked like a drowned cat, but otherwise, he seemed fine. When he stood, they stood around each other, admiring the new amulet that they'd found.

"Well, hello there..." a creepy voice called up to them suddenly, causing the four travellers to jump, turning toward it. "We'll be taking that treasure of yours, now."

It was the bandits. They had escaped.

CHAPTER XVIII

At the base of the temple, a good twenty feet below them, the bandits stood. They nearly surrounded the entire area; their ranks seemed to have doubled since the canyon. The wave of black shifted below them, maybe fifty or more men with their faces covered and their eyes glinting maliciously between the gaps in their masks.

Tobias nursed the idea that they wouldn't get out, though the thought made him sick to his stomach because, with their two best warriors drained of energy from escaping the temple's final trap, they surely wouldn't be able to fight them off.

"I said," the leader reiterated, "We'll be taking that treasure of yours, now."

"Uh, no thanks. I quite like it where it is," Ava replied, which caused Axel to give a bark of laughter.

CHAPTER XVIII

Immediately, the bandits charged, breaking ranks to storm up the side of the temple. The stairs along all four sides of the ancient building lead up where the four travellers stood, completely boxed in. Ava, in a desperate move, touched her amulet and became ghostlike once more, running toward the bandits. Their swords and fists swept right through her, though each of her attacks were solid hits.

Axel took Meredith's hand the two of them became invisible, sneaking through the crowd to cause mischief. They jumped into the fray, the only evidence of their existence in the form of bandits tripping at random, falling to the ground from an invisible force shoving them.

Finally, Tobias, having regained a little of his strength, stayed at the top of the temple, his eyes glowing with power as he began targeting the bandits with iron weapons. He could only control a few at a time, but he used that to his full advantage, changing their form. He melted the blades of the swords into a ball of liquid, bubbling and writhing in the air before it splashed to their feet. Tobias then allowed it to harden again, and the bandits were trapped, unable to move. And strangely, despite the metal's liquid form, it did not burn. Cool to the touch, the bandits only struggled against the thickness and solidity of it.

He trapped most of the bandits with the metal of their swords, leaving them to hold the useless hilts of their weapons as they pulled desperately at their feet, which were enclosed in hardened puddles of metal. By the time Tobias fell to his knees again in exhaustion, there were only twenty or so bandits remaining, most of which had been knocked down once or twice already by Ava, but she was quickly tiring as well.

She was fighting, quickly improving with her amulet, but sweat dripped down her face from the strain of using it for so long in sporadic bursts. She was still limited to making her entire body intangible or not, but by fighting them, intangible for defence and tangible for offence, she was beginning to run solely on the adrenaline that rushed through her veins.

There were fifteen bandits remaining - including the leader - all of whom were fighting with their fists. Ava knew that she could no longer use her amulet to fight, but with what little energy she had left, she charged, brandishing her dagger.

Tobias pushed himself to his feet and took slow steps down the stairs. He grabbed a spear from a fallen bandit but was so tired that he could do little more than lean on it for support.

They could not win.

Behind the line of bandits, Axel and Meredith appeared, the girl supporting her companion. Axel sat, trying to regain his energy from holding his power so long over the two of them, but Meredith followed her father's example, grabbing a spear and swished it in front of her, struggling to hold it upright. She charged into battle as well, ready to fight.

Ava, with the last of her strength, took down most of the remaining men, but Meredith was close behind, the reach of her spear giving an advantage against the bare-handed bandits who she fought.

It wasn't enough. She fell.

Not long after, Tobias felt hands wrap around his arms, forcing him to the ground as ropes were tied around his wrists. The bandits, after tying him, threw him to the ground, Meredith and Axel soon joining him, also bound. The leader approached Ava and seized the amulet from around her neck, but as he went to put it on, the gem burned. Its red light illuminated the day, stained the surrounding area in its glow.

"Ahh!" the bandit leader hissed, dropping the amulet. His hands shook in the air to cool them as blisters formed all over his palms, red and throbbing.

"What's going on, boss?" another bandit asked. As one of the few bandits remaining conscious from the fight, he'd been the one to tie Tobias, and then he'd grabbed Ava to tie her as well.

"It's hot, you imbecile! Look what it's done to me!" The leader displayed his hands, the wounds an angry red and already covered swelling masses as his body tried to heal him.

Meanwhile, Ava worked on the tight knots behind her back. Her chest was heaving from the battle, and sweat dripped off her heavily, leaving sticky trails down her body.

With one final tug, she pulled the knot loose, thanking the gods that the bandit was horrid at fastening prisoners securely, and she jumped to her feet, bringing one leg up to hit the leader in the face, sending him sprawling in the dirt.

The other bandit - the one who had tied her and the others - lunged, but she made quick work of him as well, using their leader as a human shield to give herself an advantage.

After each of the bandits had been defeated, Ava dropped the man she was holding and for the second time, the four companions defeated the bandits, though with magic on their side to even the numbers.

Standing over the unconscious bandit leader, Ava said, "I guess we can take down the emperor now."

Meredith turned to her, an affronted look on her face. "But we don't have all four amulets!" she protested. She wanted her own ability to use so that she could be of some use to them, to be an equal member of the team. She was desperate to prove herself, and she just had – fighting against bandits. For a fourteen-year-old with no previous experience, she did well.

CHAPTER XVIII

Ava rounded on her. "Where is it going to be, huh? We've looked everywhere we can! We weren't even sure that we were going to find this one-" she motioned to her own, where it rested on her chest, glowing slightly, "Before Axel found that map! Three out of four is good enough to take out one of them!"

"But Alfred said that we need all the amulets to beat the emperor. Remember, he's been using his for years. We've had ours a few days at best. We should definitely try to find the last one before going back," Tobias said, coming to his daughter's defence. He was standing almost fully on his own, but still, let a bit of his weight hang on the spear.

"Okay, genius. Where are we going to find said amulet?" Ava replied, hands on her hips as they stared at Tobias, expecting an answer.

"Um…" he said, pausing.

Ava spoke again without even letting him finish, "Exactly! I say we just go back to Arbane and give it a shot."

The others can't argue with that, so they follow her as she stormed off.

"Oi! North is tha' way!" Axel said, holding his compass out, pointing to Ava's left. Ava stopped, harrumphed, and changed directions, still stomping as she walked.

CHAPTER XIX

O n their path, the dark forest loomed overhead; the tree's forebodingly bare trunks were coarse with bark and only the very tops were bursting with dark olive-green needles. As it came into view for the four travellers, night had fallen, eclipsing the previous light of day in shadows. By the stars, Meredith led them, and they angled toward the constellation that she knew hung directly above the city.

At the edge of the forest, Meredith was surprised to see a hooded figure standing there as if waiting for them. Of course, she knew that the others must've been intrigued by the stranger as well, but she couldn't tell just by the looks on their faces. Ava's was blank, easily hiding her inner thoughts. Her father's face was pensive, a look she knew well, but she could never discern what he was thinking just by his "thinking"

CHAPTER XIX

face. Axel, overall, just looked bored, as if the sudden appearance of the man at the woods was expected.

The stranger was tall and held nothing in his hands, but Meredith saw Ava prepare herself for an attack. She did the same, as did the boys, because it had been a long few days, and suspicion had kept them alive until that point, so they weren't about to assume anyone they met was safe. He seemed harmless enough, but then again, so had Alfred, and Meredith speculated that the old man of the mountain could kill them all easily if he wanted to.

As they stood in their battle stances, forms stiff and weapons held firmly, yet aloof, the man raised his hand slowly, urging them to relax. "I am here in peace." His voice was low and calm, comforting even. Then, he reached into his pocket, pulling out a final amulet, this one with a green gem. It was an emerald, but from within, it glowed a deep, forest green, as if emanating the rich life of the conifers just ahead of them.

"Who are you?" Ava demanded, holding her dagger at him threateningly, despite his assurance that he was no threat. Her voice was harsh and distrusting, but Meredith just assumed that it came with the job. No one was an assassin for most of their life and stayed living if they couldn't learn to be suspicious of others. It was a sad thought, really, in Meredith's opinion. She hoped to be the person that Ava could learn to trust, in the future.

Realizing that she was becoming distracted, Meredith returned her focus to the peculiar man in front of them, paying close attention to his bizarre appearance.

The stranger – a tall, bald man with grey, wispy eyebrows, colourless eyes, and a hooked nose – ignored her question. Instead, he said, "I see that you're headed back to Arbane to defeat the emperor, so I will offer you this deal. If you can answer my riddle, you may take the final amulet and be on your way, but if not, you must go on and defeat him without the help of the final piece."

"Why not just give it to us?" Meredith questioned. Without being able to see it, she knew her eyebrows were higher than normal, showing her curiosity clearly on her face. Why couldn't he? If he wanted the emperor gone just as much as they did, and he knew they needed all four amulets, why couldn't he just give it to them? Why the test?

The stranger shook his head, eyes closed as he looked down at the grass, which was already becoming speckled with crisp orange-brown needles. "Alas, I cannot. As guardian of the amulet, I must abide by the laws of magic. It will only yield its command to another if it is won in a challenge – a test of the mind. Therefore, you must answer me these three riddles correctly, and it will obey your command."

CHAPTER XIX

As her curiosity became quenched, Meredith perked up at the stranger's words. She was the last to receive an amulet, and as a consistent solver of riddles, she knew that she had the best chance to win the amulet's control from the stranger. It had to be fate.

"We will take your challenge," Tobias said. His bright blue eyes were confident, and he spoke knowing that his daughter would have the answers, and finally receive an amulet of her own. Seeing it caused immense pride to surge through Meredith, and she sent a quick smile toward her father.

"My first riddle is as follows: Turn us on our backs / And open up our stomachs / You will be the wisest of men / Though at start a lummox."

Meredith smiled, her brain quickly putting the pieces together. "This is an easy one," she claimed.

"If it is so easy, my dear, then what, pray tell, is the answer?"

With a grin, the teen gave her answer. "Books. The answer is books. They are the object opened on their backs and give the knowledge of man to all with their contents."

The stranger smiled. "Very good. But this is only the first. My second riddle, now. Prepare yourself. Never ahead, ever behind / Yet flying swiftly past / For a child I last forever / For adults I'm gone too fast. What am I now, child?" he asked with a sly twinkle in his eyes.

Meredith's eyebrows furrowed. That riddle was harder, for sure. What could it be? She turned to the others.

"I dunno," Axel said with a shrug. Obviously, he wouldn't have been Meredith's first choice at a literary problem such as a riddle. Instead, the teen girl turned to her father.

"What do you think, dad?"

The older man just smiled down at his daughter. "I believe that it is something that I've long since lost, and you, though are still entitled to it, have lost it in these past days as well. It is not something that I wished upon you; I am only glad that you've had so many years of it before, still happy, even without your mother by your side."

Meredith's eyes widened as her father finished his hint. Of course! She spun around, facing the old stranger one again. "For your second riddle, my answer is childhood."

Blackened teeth glared at her from his smile. "You have answered two out of my three questions correctly. Well done. Revel in this, for not many have achieved as such. However, this last riddle of mine is the most intricate of them all. It will also describe an object, in case that part seems unclear when you hear it. Your only task is to tell me what this object is. Are you ready?"

CHAPTER XIX

Meredith nodded. "We're ready; tell us your final riddle."

Clearing his throat, the stranger began, "A serpent swam in a silver urn / A gold bird did in its mouth abide / The serpent drank the water, this in turn / Killed the serpent. Then the gold bird died." He paused after telling them his riddle, allowing them time to repeat the words in their heads. "Take your time," he suggested, "But I advise you be quick about it. Remaining here in the open is a dangerous move."

Turning to huddle together, the four travellers tried to come up with the answer. The stranger remained silent after that, waiting patiently for the answer to his riddle. He knew that only the one worthy of receiving the final amulet would be able to produce the answer by sheer wit alone, and he so desperately hoped that the chosen one was among their group.

"Wha' is 'e even askin'?" Axel inquired. His head was tilted to the side, affectionately reminding Meredith of a puppy, but she quickly pushed the thought aside.

"I don't know," Ava replied, her voice quiet as she spoke aloud, more to herself than anyone else, "Maybe we have to use the clues to figure out what it is that he's talking about? I bet the serpent and the bird are metaphors for something or another."

"What's a metaphor?" Axel asked, though this time his question was ignored.

"Well, what has a thing that dies if another thing dies?" Tobias asked, completely clueless. The variables in his statement only made it all the more confusing.

Meredith, who remained silent during their discussion, was deep in thought. She knew that she had to be the one to answer the question to have control of the amulet. The others had all proved themselves – more or less – and she had to do the same.

If only she could figure out what it was.

She most certainly agreed that the serpent and the bird were metaphors, but for what? A gold bird…a gold bird… Typically, in her books, the gold bird of the land was a phoenix, so maybe…fire? Could it mean fire?

If the gold bird was fire, and there was a serpent in an urn… She ran the lines through her head once more. A serpent swam in a silver urn / A gold bird did in its mouth abide / The serpent drank the water, this in turn / Killed the serpent. Then the gold bird died. There was water involved, or maybe not, but once it was gone…the bird died. The flame? She was having trouble keeping up with her thoughts.

Leaving the group, she knelt in the dirt and began to trace a small box in the soft loam. It was a container, with a snake within, swimming around. Tracing the snake's mouth with gaping jaws, facing up, she pressed her finger into the dirt for a small dot to signify the flame. To top it off, she drew a small squiggle within the "urn" to represent the water. Staring at the image, Meredith tilted her head, squinting as she inspected it. Then, her eyes widened, and she drew one last piece – a curved glass casing – around the small flame.

Meredith smiled nervously. She had her answer.

When she approached the stranger with her answer, she felt suddenly timid, and the confidence she felt about her answer waned a little. "It is an oil lamp?" she asked, hands rubbing over one another as she anticipated the verification of her response.

Her voice was quiet, but the man didn't say anything about it. He looked down at her. "Are you asking me or telling me?" he asked in return.

Meredith paused, before collecting her voice. "Telling," she decided, her tone becoming much more confident, "The answer to your riddle is an oil lamp."

The stranger didn't move for a moment, but then his mouth curved into a smile under his hooked nose. "Well done," he said. He then held out the amulet, which had gone dark, but when he placed it in her hand, wrapping her fingers around it, the gem lit up once again in a brilliant bright green light. "Treasure it, always. With this, you will gain the ability to manipulate shadows to your will. It is a fair power to have and will be the key in vanquishing the emperor."

Meredith nodded and called out to the others. "Let's go!"

As they passed him, she paused, turning back as she realized that she hadn't even thanked the man for his help. "Thank-" her voice wavered. The man was gone. Meredith stood there, confused for a moment. She looked left and right, eyes searching the trees for a sign of his cloak, but there was none.

"Meredith! Come on, we're leaving!" her father called, his voice slightly muffled by the distance that he'd put between them. Looking around once more, Meredith shrugged, dashing away to join her three companions.

CHAPTER XX

Continuing their journey through the forest, the four travellers trekked late into the night, luckily still able to see the stars above through the foliage. As they walked along, the ground grew soggier, and they stopped at the swamp that rested in the direct centre of the forest. The swamp had one large pond, with a single land bridge leading through the middle of it, which seemed to be the only way to cross without going all the way around.

"Arbane lies just on the opposite side of this swamp," Ava stated, "I've never been here, myself, but it seems a good a place to go as any, and it'll shorten our trip by at least a day from having to walk all the way around."

Axel was about to cross when suddenly: "Stop right there!" The voice was loud and grouchy, rolled off the tongue of a man who obviously didn't get many visitors. His accent was strange, different than anything Axel had heard before. His head turned, and he saw an angry-looking man in overalls and a muddy tunic emerge from the undergrowth. He carried a shovel in one hand, had a small stalk of wheat that he twirled between his teeth, and the scowl on his face seemed to be permanently stuck there.

"If you're gonna pass through my swamp, I demand you pay the toll! This is my land, and you must pay a fine to walk upon it," he said, his hand outstretched in an obvious demand of their coinage.

Axel wasn't just about to pay the grouch with his last gold coin. He'd worked hard to steal those from the dragon's cave, and after the rest had been sacrificed to keep Tobias from drowning in quicksand, he'd keep the last one as a souvenir for the rest of his natural days. He certainly wasn't going to give anything to the farmer, whose black hair was splattered with grease and mud, and whose brown eyes stared into his soul like a demon.

"Who are you?" Ava asked the man, and though her polite tone sounded false to Axel, the farmer didn't seem to notice.

"I'm Logan, and this land belongs to me. If ya wanna use 'em, you gotta pay a fee," he drawled.

CHAPTER XX

"Well...you see-" Tobias was about to explain but was cut off by another voice emerging from the surrounding forest.

"You cannot lay claim to the terrain of Mother Earth! This land belongs to no man!" The second time a person appeared, it was a woman, seemingly in her late-twenties, and wielding a lengthy sword barring an elegant handle. She wore pristine clothing, somehow remaining clean in the slums of the swamp.

"Who'd'ya think you are?" Logan demanded as he stomped toward the woman.

"I am Rose, obviously, old man, as I've always been. You cannot stop people from crossing the swamp; they will always come, but you have no right to charge them!" the woman – Rose – replied.

"Why I outta-!" Logan said before raising his shovel in a threatening move. He swung the weapon at Rose, who countered with her sword. They exchanged blows, sword against shovel, and by their movements, Axel could tell that they'd fought often.

As he watched the two, strange people, Axel let out a laugh – something that he hadn't done in what felt like months, especially with the events of the past few days running through his mind. He didn't even realise how much he'd needed to laugh until the boisterous bellows were spilling from his lips and his stomach began to hurt from the strain.

A slap to his arm did little to stop his laughter, but he did hear Ava hiss in his ear. "Come one! Let's sneak by them while they're not watching. We still have a quest to fulfill, don't we?"

Those were the words that got Axel moving. He nodded, stifling his laughter a little – but only a little – and did as Ava suggested.

As the two were distracted, Ava grabbed Meredith's and Tobias' hands and led them away, leaving Axel to follow as they snuck away from the quarrelling rivals. Axel's feet squelched loudly in the mud, as did the others' shoes, and with each step, he was worried he'd find Logan around his shoulder, demanding his gold, or Rose with her sword, demanding his life, but that never happened.

His worry remained, however, until they left the swamp behind, and returned to the dry greenery of the forest, whose greens were much brighter than the dullness of the swamp. After the final stretch of trees, there was only one obstacle left in their path on the way to Arbane. A final canyon, which was a short walk, carrying no ill will in its crags.

"Ha!" she exclaimed as they were finally back out in the open. "Tha' was a good laugh, huh? Two weirdos comin' ou', one demandin' our money, an' the other demandin' we don't pay? Then them fightin' over i', so focused tha' they don't even see us leave! Ha! Wha' a thrill! I needed tha'! Really!" he let out another bellow of laughter, followed by a breathy guffaw.

Meredith giggled a little, and even Ava let out a chuckle, then Tobias.

"Yeah... That was pretty funny, wasn't it? What was even the point of those two if they can't agree on anything? I mean, why do they even live in a swamp?" Ava asked. Her questions would forever remain unanswered, so she brushed them aside shortly after they were said.

Their journey would continue, and finally, they'd face the closing of their quest: facing the emperor.

Across the open plains was the city of Arbane, standing tall and facetious against the midday sky. Axel rounded back past the last corner of the canyon, pulling the others with him. "We gotta plan how we're gonna get in," he suggested.

"Well, one of us can become invisible, and the other can control shadows. That's two ways for us to be unseen. Axel, you and Tobias turn invisible and I say you just walk through the front gate. Meredith and I will sneak in through the walls. We'll meet you in the emperor's throne room."

Axel nodded, and he pulled his gold coins out of his pockets and handed them to Tobias. "Pu' these in the bag an' leave it 'ere. We'll get it later." Tobias nodded and pulled the bag over his shoulder, allowing Axel to drop the coins in before finding a well-hidden niche in the wall of the cliff to store it.

With his powers, he clasped Tobias' hand and with the other, touched his fingers to the golden gem of his amulet. They became unseen, which allowed for easy access past the guards and through the gate into the main city.

"We're takin' back alleys," Axel whispered to Tobias once they were inside the city.

"Definitely," Tobias agreed, "If we go down the main road, we'll surely be knocked into and discovered." Sneaking through the front entrance of the palace after navigating the winding back routes of the city – which Axel still knew like the back of his hand – they crossed the courtyard and entered the palace. From that point on, Tobias led the way, his expertise with the layout of the palace even more so than Axel's with the streets.

Entering the throne room on one of the higher floors, Axel dropped his power, making them visible just as the two boys saw a shadow emerging from the wall, the darkness fading to reveal Ava and Meredith. All four of them looking to the far wall, they saw the emperor, Absinthe. He was lounging on his throne, somewhat lazily, popping grapes into his mouth every so often. When he saw them, he smirked, and jumped up from his throne, surprisingly agile for his age.

CHAPTER XX

"My, my," he said. His voice was deep and held confidence and power at a level that Axel could never hope to achieve. "What do we have here?"

Without waiting for an answer, the emperor drew the sword from his belt and charged. Their battle ensued. By the end, one of the adversaries would be captured or dead, and the victor would have the power to achieve absolute control over the kingdom. They could not let him win.

CHAPTER XXI

Ava felt a rapid quiver in her chest as she anticipated the fight, the bejewelled dagger clutched tightly in her left hand, raised as she ran across the long room, the soles of her shoes slapping loudly against the wood floor, which was so polished that her warped reflection ran below similarly prepared for battle. In the space between her and the emperor, Ava's mind wandered back to the days previous, of the journey that began when Axel had convinced Tobias and Meredith to help save her from a gruesome fate. It had only been a few days, but to her, it felt longer than the past few months of her life combined.

First, she thought of the mountain with that strange old man – Alfred – and his many, many books. The fruit that he'd offered her, which ran out before they'd reached the oasis, had been so sweet and juicy, unlike anything she'd tasted before. There was the healing of her ribs done by the sanctuary, a magic that she'd never thought of, but was still immensely grateful for. Then, before the haven that was the sparkling blue and lush green of the oasis, there were the long days they had spent out in the Uvian desert, under the burning sun that somehow felt hotter there than any other area in the kingdom. She thought of the dragon in its cave, which they left to its treasure after purloining the magic dagger she now wielded, and the second amulet used by Tobias. The poor reptile that probably would never leave as it had grown too large to escape the cramped confines of the earth. It would die, and come back, as all dragons did, from its own ashes, rising to live and defend its horde – a dragon's pride and joy.

Then, midway across the room, Ava saw Absinthe pause, bringing his hand up to his amulet. Her heart stopped. Oh no. If he used his power, any one of them was at risk. There had to be a way to stop him from controlling them, but what? Blackness overtook his eyes, as did his amulet, and unlike the rest of them, the glow of his power burned brighter, outlining his whole body. It surged around him like a black flame, writhing in the air as if struggling to escape his form for bigger deeds. The emperor stared directly at Tobias, causing the latter to freeze in place. Around the poor man, the darkness lunged, striking venomously like a viper and injecting its poison.

Ava kept running. She only heard her footsteps on the floor and the blood rushing through her ears. Tunnel vision showed her the emperor where he stood, his gaze focused elsewhere, giving her the opportunity that she needed. He was distracted, so she could strike, and he would fall.

He would fall.

She circled around, keeping herself out of his view as to keep the upper hand.

Unfortunately, she only saw half of what the emperor was doing, because, by the time she'd reached him, about to attack from behind, he was ready. Before she could bring the dagger down on his shoulder, Absinthe turned to her and Tobias' attention shifted. Her friend's eyes – void of any emotion – rested on Ava where she stood, and his hand shot up, pointing toward her.

Suddenly, an iron chain flew across the room, colliding with Ava's neck; it wrapped around her like a noose, lifting her in the air by her throat. The chain was tight against her flesh, holding almost lovingly, and yet it was killing her. She choked, gagging rasps escaping her lips, but little more was heard. Her feet kicked out, body writhing in an effort to free herself, to no avail.

To save her, Meredith quickly jumped forward as Axel moved to land a hit on Absinthe from behind. The young girl's efforts were futile as she tugged at the chains that her father was slowly tightening around Ava, achieving nothing but pulling the noose tighter.

Instead, she changed her tactics.

"Ava, I'm going to try something," she said, already focusing her power as she spoke. "It might not work, but if it does, be prepared for the chain to let go. You're going to fall."

Ava barely managed to nod her head to prove that she'd heard – because any movement brought her closer to death. Black spots danced before her eyes and her head felt light, like a balloon on the end of its string, tied loosely to the earth. Any moment and she'd fly away, forever lost in the atmosphere.

Between the spots of darkness, she saw Meredith go about her plan, though was unable to decipher what the girl was doing.

Using shadows, Meredith sent streaks of her power toward her father, the darkness wrapping around his eyes like fabric, blinding him. Seconds after, Tobias' body stilled, tensed, relaxed, and tensed again. Immediately, the chain's grip slackened, and fell limply from Ava's neck. Without the support, she fell to the ground and despite preparing herself for the landing, she fell in a heap.

A weak smile graced her lips as she looked up at the teen. The plan worked! Tobias was freed and in turn, Ava would live. Placing her hands underneath her, the assassin pushed herself up, her chest heaved a lungful of glorious air – something she always took for granted. Not anymore, she vowed silently.

Meanwhile, Tobias steadied himself where he stood, blinking. "What happened?" he asked, still blinded. He brought his hands up to his face, unable to feel anything, but also unable to see. The efforts to rub away dirt or debris was all for nought, as no matter how hard he tried, his vision would not return.

"Dad!" Meredith ran over to him. Her voice was loud and panicked, which seemed counterintuitive to what she was trying to do. "Calm down! My shadows are blinding you because the emperor took you over! If you can't see him, he can't control you. Just listen to my voice and I'll guide you."

He nodded.

"Do you trust me?" Her voice, no longer timid as she spoke. There was a confidence that Tobias had never heard before as she asked him for control over his attacks – as she asked him to give her his power.

Tobias nodded, touching his amulet once again to power it up. He could just barely see the outlines of the room, but everything was a blur.

"To your left!" he heard his daughter yell, and his hand moved, controlling whatever iron in the vicinity and sending it where she directed. There was a loud cry, and Tobias hoped to the gods that he'd hit the emperor. If not...that was bad.

Meanwhile, Ava felt shadows wrap around her eyes as well, done by Meredith to protect her from falling under the emperor's control. She fought him, using her other senses to guide her. Focusing on the sound of Absinthe's breathing and his footsteps, she was able to avoid his attacks, meeting him blow for blow. He was out of shape and out of practice, she could tell, because sitting on a throne without anyone to oppose him had done nothing to keep up his abilities with a sword.

Still, he managed to knock her dagger aside, though she did the same with his sword, and they fought hand to hand until finally, she had him in a hold, one arm behind him while the other was around his own neck, squeezing the life out of him. Axel took his chance to grab the amulet from around the emperor's neck, but as soon as he felt the tug, the emperor broke free with one of his hands and grabbed the amulet as it was removed from him, sending it to the ground.

Upon colliding with the floor, the amulet burst into pieces, the gem scattered into millions of tiny fragments across the polished wood. The glow of the gem faded instantly, but as soon as the first crack appeared, pure, unaltered energy surged forth, unleashed into the world, and the throne room shook.

CHAPTER XXII

I n hindsight, breaking one of the five most valuable artifacts – one of the most powerful magical items – in the known world seemed like a bad idea, but at the time, they didn't have a choice. It fell. It broke. Simple as that.

Once the pieces came to rest on the wooden boards, the whole world shivered. Bright flashes of black light from the amulet escaped with haste from its pieces, like dark spirits fleeing their cage after millennia of imprisonment. They vanished, free in the world, but no one had the time to consider what it meant as the destruction continued. Each piece of glass vibrated, and they too began shattering, breaking further and further until nothing but fine dust was left, almost impossible to spot along the floor.

Around the four travellers, the palace trembled, and their amulets, though the use of their powers was over, began to glow, pulsing with energy – like Absinthe's had. Each of them glowed with their own colour, as it always had been, but the brighter they were, the purer the colour became. Axel's glowed gold, matching the gold which he so loved. Ava's was red to reflect her personality and the heat of the fire which burned within her. Tobias' was blue, as was his soul, of sadness, but also deep calm, and finally, Meredith's glowed green, the bright, happy colour of the open meadows that she so adored.

"What's happenin'?" Axel yelled, panicked, as the shaking grew stronger, the four of them knocked to the floor. Ava remained by Absinthe's side, holding him beneath her so he couldn't escape.

"Didn't Alfred tell us something about breaking the amulets? I can't remember! What did he say?" Meredith shouted her question in reply.

"Probably not to break them!" Ava screamed, unable to fathom why they were discussing it when it was obviously bad.

"But then what do we do?" Tobias asked.

"Alfred mentioned that the five amulets co-exist in harmony! Maybe since one of them is broken, the others' powers are unbalanced!" Meredith suggested.

"Are you saying we have to break ours to stop the shaking?" Ava demanded. As the shaking intensified, she struggled to keep her grip on the emperor.

Axel was the first to smash his. He pulled it from over his head and threw it to the ground. It shattered but did nothing but cause the other three to glow brighter. "Uh oh!" he shouted. "Tha' seemed like a bad idea!"

"No! Keep going! Once they're all destroyed, the shaking should stop!" Meredith said.

"You fools!" the emperor cried as Meredith grabbed her own amulet and Ava's preparing herself to shatter them as well. "You are only destroying your powers! If you smash the amulets, you will never have these abilities again!"

His voice was barely heard as the trembling reached its peak. The room was visibly shaking, decorations coming off the walls and cracks appearing in the floor, separating Ava and Absinthe from the others. However, Tobias ignored the emperor's words as he took his – the last amulet – and threw it to the ground. It splintered, pieces scattering and dissolving until there was no trace.

In fact, none of them left a trace.

With one final shudder, the earthshaking ceased. Though, using the shaking to his advantage, Absinthe freed his arm, throwing it at Ava and managing to escape her grasp as she fell back against the floor, momentarily stunned.

CHAPTER XXII

Scrambling to his feet, he ran, undignified, toward the entrance in a desperate attempt to bolt. Throwing the doors open, he was about to flee, only to see the guards standing there, a little dishevelled, but free of his control. Their chainmail was askew, and their spears and swords were held aloft, but as soon as they saw the emperor, anger overtook their confusion and their hands took ahold of their former slaver, forcing him to the ground. The fallen emperor knelt, scowling at the ground before they hoisted him into their firm grasps.

The two of them led him to the dungeons – a place he'd sent so many to their deaths – while two other guards walk into the throne room, seeing the four companions still inside, on the ground and ready to collapse from exhaustion for the umpteenth time since the beginning of their journey.

"What happened here?" one of the guards asked, "And who are you?"

Axel, who was the only one with enough breath in his lungs to speak properly, stepped forward to explain, "I'm Axel. These 're ma friends, and we just got rid of the emperor's blasted amulet, so I guess yer all free now." He ended his statement with a shrug, then sniffled and swiped at his nose to send away an itch.

*

Upon securing the ex-emperor in what used to be his own dungeons, the guards returned, and all looked to Axel. "Now that Absinthe has been overthrown, we will need a new emperor," he said, "Will you or any of your friends take the position?"

Axel looked around at the others, then turned back to the guards. "Nah," he said, "We don't need that kind 'a power. It would get to our heads, so best leave the emperor business to someone else. Better yet, have no emperor! Tha's too much power fer one person."

The guards' eyebrows furrowed as they stared at him in confusion. "What do you mean, no emperor?" the head guard asked.

"Have a council ta run ev'rythin'. We'll make decisions t'gether and it'll be better than one guy tellin' ev'ryone wha' ta do," he elaborated.

"In that case, we'll assign you as a high minister, and your friends will be..." the head guard trailed off, his eyes wandering to the others.

"Make 'em 'ead o' security, 'ead architect, an' 'ead as'ronomer," Axel replied, knowing his friends well enough to know what they'd want. Looking at them again, he was met with smiles.

And so, the changes were made. Axel became a high minister, the mouthpiece of the council. He would be the one speaking to the people, once his education was completed, and he'd travel around from city to town to village, inspecting how things were going around the kingdom.

Ava, another member of the council, left her life as an assassin for hire to take charge over the guards. She abandoned her original plan to flee the kingdom in favour of the position, and almost immediately fell into it with ease.

Once again, Tobias took up the helm as chief architect. He moved toward rebuilding the castle first, making places for people to stay with their families while he continued his work, rebuilding the lower town after the destruction that the recent earthquakes wracked upon the houses of the city folk.

Meredith was given a position on the council as well and became an astronomer, as was her dream, alongside a kind man named Marcus, who was more experienced and taught her much more than she'd ever learned from her books. She and Marcus became co-chiefs of the position and began their project of mapping the night sky.

*

Despite the joyous ending to their journey, not all ended in success. Only days after securing their new positions, a guard barged into the first ever meeting of the council, his pace frantic and the expression he wore saturated in worry.

"What's going on?" Ava asked, immediately on her feet, the chair pushed back with a loud screech.

"The emperor-I mean..." the guard paused, unable to formulate words. "He's escaped! He's gone!" he managed.

The others were up as well, more chairs screeching. Tobias' was knocked over with a thundering clatter.

"How? What is the meaning of this?" he demanded.

The guard shifted nervously; his eyebrows were furrowed, and his shoulders hunched to give his stature an air of paranoia. Obviously, he didn't hold himself together well under pressure. "I... I don't know. I..."

"Why don't you just lead us to the dungeons and we'll see for ourselves," Meredith interrupted the man's stuttering, though her voice held only serenity, not a trace of anger present. Her heart still beat rapidly in her chest at the revelation of this new development, but she saw no use in taking out her frustrations on the messenger.

"Oh, yes! Right!" the poor guard hopped in place once, trying to straighten his back to regain at least a little dignity, and turned to lead them to the dungeons.

They of course, already knew the way, but there was no need to tell him that, as he seemed so determined to do his job well.

CHAPTER XXII

As they arrived, it seemed that the guard was right. The cell was empty, the door open, though there was no obvious tampering to the lock. There was nothing but the thin hay mattress and the bucket in the corner, illuminated by the sunlight coming through the small barred window on the opposite wall.

Well, there was something.

On the wall, in a thick red substance, was a message. Below it was the body of another guard, dead and staring into the middle distance.

"It's blood," Axel said solemnly as he knelt next to the guard to close his eyes. He nodded to the message. "Some'ne read it, will ya?"

Tobias cleared his throat to rid himself of the lump that formed there. "It says I will get my revenge. This kingdom shall be mine again."

"Well, that's not foreboding at all," Ava muttered. She received an elbow to the ribs from Meredith. "Hey! Watch it!"

"Shh!" Meredith hissed. "A man is dead! Have a little more respect!"

Ava scowled, looking like she wanted to say something – probably about how she used to kill people for a living – but went against her first instinct. Instead, she remained silent.

"What do we do now?" Tobias asked. "The emperor is still out there, then we have to be on our toes at all times. If he attacks, we need to be ready." He turned to Axel, who stood, though his eyes were still downcast.

"It's not if 'e attacks, it's when. We 'ave ta defend the city. Star' the repair plans."

*

Axel sat in his office after months of settling into his new role. Rolling the tension out of his shoulders, he straightened in his chair. After classes every day since they defeated the emperor, he had taken to remaking the map, inserting everything that he and his friends had learned from their journey throughout the eastern lands of Ghanara. He was certain that as the ambassador, he would have many more adventures throughout the kingdom he had been made responsible for, and he looked forward to every trip ahead.

In the meantime, his office was where he spent most of his time, so it was as comfortable as he could make it. There were shelves lining the walls; after he'd learned to read, it had become a favoured past time of his. In the centre stood a wooden desk, fashioned for him with many drawers and a wide-open space for him to display his possessions as he worked.

On the desk, while he studied, there were always a select few items that he appreciated by his side. Firstly, the old pocket watch that he'd snatched those many weeks ago – a watch that didn't work but marked a sentimental value for him as the beginning of his journey with his newfound friends: Ava, Tobias, and Meredith. The second was his compass. Looking at the latter item again, he cast his eyes over the map in front of him one last time before – with a final nod of approval – he rolled it up and placed it aside. Seconds later, the compass was in his hands as he stood. He'd had the compass for many years, ever since the day that his father had given it to him, and he'd kept it in the best condition, but ever since the final battle, he could no longer use it for its purpose.

During the quake, his compass had fallen, and the glass cracked as it collided with the floor, the needle snapped in half behind the protective casing. However, the picture was still okay, and that was all Axel cared about as he set it on the shelf in the corner, open-faced so that his parents and younger self could smile out at the office.

Axel smiled as well. It was almost as if they were there with him, seeing the happiness that he'd found with his new life. He may have started out as an orphan with nothing, but by the end of his story, he lived a comfortable life with the responsibility to keep everyone around him comfortable as well.Leaving it there, he allowed his feet to lead him out on the balcony above the courtyard to greet the city folk.

"Hello!" he shouted. "I'm proud to announce that the restoration of the lower town shall begin soon! The blueprints are done, and we'll begin work within the week!"

A cheer rose from down below, and Axel smiled, feeling as if the sound of unaltered happiness was lifting him, higher than the balcony ever could. His heart felt lighter in his chest and the flutter of joy sent a comfortable shiver down his spine.

24764084R00124

Made in the USA
Columbia, SC
29 August 2018